AMALIE

BY

E.J. WOOD

AMALIE   E.J. WOOD

Black Cat Books

Amalie by E.J. Wood

BOOKS BY EJ WOOD

Beyond the Pale
Amalie
The Kidnapper's Word – Book 1 DCI
The Forgotten Man

'You are so brave and quiet, I forget you are suffering.'

Ernest Hemingway

~

Let's never forget.

For the one I love, this one is for you.

I

BERKSHIRE, ENGLAND

PROLOGUE

BROADMOOR HOSPITAL
The year is 1980

You call me crazy, a monster and many other derogatory names. You see, the authorities see me as a problem they cannot solve. Their easy way out would be to bury me in a concrete coffin; out of sight, out of mind. It doesn't matter to them the reasons behind my actions, they don't know the answers, and they don't really care.

My life in solitary is unbroken depression. My furnishings consist of soft compressed cardboard, I imagine so I don't hurt myself? Or is it for your safety? And my sink and lavatory are bolted to the floor next to a concrete slab as my bed; things haven't improved in the last forty years then?

I'm left to vegetate and regress, but with no one listening what's the point? Isn't the idea of solitary confinement just that? Solitary...

"To see a world in a grain of sand, and a heaven in a wild flower",' and all... Had the English poet William Blake foreseen the cruelties and barbarism against innocents when he wrote Auguries of Innocence back in 1803? Pitting rich against poor, innocent against mature, all opposites to show hypocrisy in contemporary life? Was he a genius or a madman? I'll let you decide.

They put me in this 6ft x 9ft cell with a Perspex wall hoping to learn about me, break me? They say if

I behave myself they will give me special privileges; I've heard *that* one before. *Just give me a cyanide tablet and be done with it!* Wouldn't that be easily and swiftly resolved, if Amalie Keller just...died?

Entertainment is rather...bleak might I add? Persuading an inmate to swallow her tongue was only light entertainment for what was it... ten minutes? Of course, that was until they moved me here. *A danger to society*...they labelled me. *She* was doomed when she said, *"I don't know what your problem is Keller, but I bet it's hard to pronounce."*

I thought it most courteous to say when the warden passed my Perspex window that, *"We're going to be one short on roll call today."* Dr Harlow didn't see the humour in it; dull bastard.

My feelings towards Dr Harlow grow increasingly with, I'm sure, a mutual hatred, and his lording over me sickens me as he tries to incompetently quantify me.

Broadmoor Hospital is for the criminally insane and those whose sanity is being evaluated. The general administrator, Dr Walter Harlow, is as pompous as they come and an incompetent director for the sanatorium that he has been assigned. His petty punishments don't go unnoticed, and his growing jealousy of my willingness to share information with law enforcement rather infuriates him, but it gives me great pleasure.

His mediocrity and self-importance make my skin crawl. I laughed out loud when I saw him on the four o'clock news boasting about new evidence now that he has a name, "Hansom Tiling," in a cold case for which he so desperately wants credit for solving. That should keep him occupied for a while. But, giving him the name gave me what I wanted, and that was access to the prison library so I can occupy myself with good quality literature. Speaking of that big bald fuck – here he comes now.

'Keller,' Dr Harlow states while standing in front of me.

'Any rational society would let me die,' I answer.

'Why would we do that? You're our most prized asset.' He grimly smiles. 'Besides, you know Capital Punishment was outlawed back in '69.'

'"Do what you will. This world is a fiction and made up of contradiction".'

'Excuse me?' Harlow asked.

'William Blake.'

'Who?' Harlow croaked.

'One of England's greatest poets of all time…. I don't really have all the crayons to explain it to you.' He looked at me with that vacant look, like the lights were on but no one was home. 'We live to die. We wage war to achieve peace. This world is a paradox.'

'Oh, Amalie, cheer up. You're so confined in your delusional thinking that you really cannot see just how monstrous you are.'

'You have no idea.'

'You still think you're going to be sipping Martinis on some beach? I don't think so, somehow. If you've been told otherwise, I'd seriously reconsider who your friends are. Now, stand facing the wall, place your hands on your head, and do not move. Understood?'

'Whatever you say, Doctor.'

'Good. You have a visitor.'

You see, way back then, when I was born, the world was just cops and robbers. Then *it* happened and the world was never the same again, and neither was I.

II

HUNGARY

CHAPTER 1

Never forget.

It was September, 1939, and so the Second World War began. Germany invaded Poland on the 1st and the USSR on the 17th.

Nine-year-old Amalie stood in the back garden with her brother Jakob. Little did they know this day was the last day before their lives irrevocably changed. Jakob, four years her senior, took Amalie's hand and pulled her towards the garden; a rich field of green velvet surrounded by splashes of red berries, the flower beds a riot of colour and weed-free. The freshly cut grass offered that summertime scent. But summer was over, and although the sun was high, the days were cooler even on days that lacked clouds.

Every day leaned towards the inevitable colder winter ahead with each night's darkness arriving sooner than the night before, and the sun would rise and set as if in a hurry to reach winter.

'Amalie, Amalie,' her brother called. They laughed as they played and she returned his smile.

'A for Amalie,' Jakob explained.

'A…malie,' she answered.

'This way, hurry,' Jakob tugged her arm.

The children giggled as they played. As the golden rays of the morning sun emerged, the birds chirped their melodious choruses, and her brother paused as their parents bellowed for them to come inside.

'Children, breakfast is ready!'

As they paused their play, the children felt the ground shudder. The distant drone of explosions rumbled across the garden, her brother grabbed her hand and they ran back home for safety.

The grass was laid out like a royal carpet with the reds and golds from the sun high above, and the children inhaled the fresh air. The trees swayed gracefully against the light wind, and the autumn breeze carried fine drops with a promise of rain.

As the children entered the yard, their father was panicked.

'Amalie, Jakob, where have you been? Hurry, quickly!'

'Jakob, come here, help me,' their mother called and the children's eyes widened with concern.

'Darling, we must go. Everything is ready, we don't have much time,' their father bellowed as he packed the cart.

'I just need help gathering the rest of my belongings, Leo, please send Jakob! I can't carry it all.'

'Jakob, help your mother, but hurry.'

Amalie climbed into the wagon as the Keller family prepared to leave everything behind, and Jakob ran upstairs to gather the rest of their belongings. As the wagon headed West, Amalie thought about the conversations she and her brother Jakob had heard; they overheard their parents discussing the rise of Nazism and the possibility of evacuation. Of course, at the time they didn't understand. Germany quickly became transformed into a totalitarian state, and nearly all aspects of life became controlled by the government. When the national referendum of 1934 confirmed Hitler as a sole leader, his word became the highest law, and racism, especially anti-Semitism, became a central ideological feature.

Amalie knew big changes were happening. Her father was home more, their food rations were much smaller, and their mother cried almost every day. Education suffered, their school was damaged by bombing, and the next nearest school had been requisitioned by the government. Young male teachers were called to fight the war, and the students were asked to help raise money for knitting comforters for the troops, a talent her mother had passed on to her.

Adolf Hitler had been a name frequently mentioned and as his Party rose in popularity, the hatred for the Jewish people increased; blaming them for the problems of Germany. Although Amalie's father was British born, her mother was Jewish, and as the hatred grew with the country's poor economic crisis, the family were forced to leave their home and everything they had come to love.

'We're moving away so we will be safe, the fighting won't be near us.' Leo whispered to the children.

Amalie's mother stroked the girl's hair.

'Don't worry, darling, it's just an adventure,' she said. 'Don't be afraid.'

The journey to Belgium was long and tiresome. As the Kellers travelled through the sylvan areas, the wind howled and blew a bitter chill. The leaves danced among the white blanket of velvet snow beneath them, and the smell of woodland decomposition and tall silhouettes offered no reassurance that the Kellers were doing the right thing; fleeing their home for a haven in a non-Nazi controlled part of Europe. As eyes all around watched them travel, it was obvious they were just as vulnerable here as when they were home, and an unnerving presence of evil lurked as if the Devil himself was waiting for the Kellers to make a mistake before he made his move and they became prey to the forest.

Living as refugees in Belgium, their father smiled more, her mother stopped crying, and Jakob and Amalie went back to school. She learned the language, made new friends, they had a new home, and life was great.

'Amalie,' Jakob smiled and attracted Amalie's attention whilst she bathed in a tin bath from the water they had heated from the large copper near the fire. Bath day was once a week, and it was this day their mother also baked fresh bread. At this point, the SS were exterminating their friends, those they left behind. People who couldn't leave with them were presumed murdered; the Germans weren't far away when their father ordered them to leave. As night-time fell, their stomachs rumbled, Father and Jakob went looking for food; the forest once plentiful of game is now quiet. The winter has moved all the animals away so they return empty-handed. Their mother prepared some vegetables she salvaged from home, but their portions were small, and Amalie noticed that her mother went without.

'We can't continue like this, Leo.' Eva whispered to her husband, hugging him close to her chest.

'I know.'

On the 10th of May, 1940, the Nazis invaded Belgium. New laws and regulations were introduced.

First came the soldiers and then came the men in black, the SS. There were loudspeakers, with speeches declaring loud and clear what they wanted.

Amalie wasn't allowed outside; they couldn't go out, watch a movie, or see friends. Her father lost his job, and they had to change schools again. The Kellers missed their old home. Here they had an outside lavatory and no bathroom to wash in. The daughter shared a bed with her brother next to their parents, and their food once again had been rationed. What food Leo could barter for, such as meat, butter, eggs, and cheese were less bountiful, and their mother tried harder to grow their own vegetables.

The air had a cold malevolent tone to it, the wind howled and explosions offered a never-ending moan. As the night fell, a dense fog rolled, lights flickered from across the field holding them in fear. They clung to each other tightly and quivered, waiting for the bullets to slaughter them like sheep.

The hairs on Amalie's neck rose like pins with the terror of it all.

'Amalie,' her brother took her hand and squeezed it, gently offering comfort.

Terror had sucked every breath from her mouth and she was unable to answer.

'It's a tank, it's the Russians!'

'Under the table,' her father shouted.

'EVERYBODY OUT!' The soldier demanded, 'Are you, Roma?'

'No.' Leo answered hugging his wife tightly and

signalling the children to be quiet.

'Are you Jews?' the soldier asked.

'Yes.' Eva proudly answered.

'Eva, no,' Leo grabbed her tightly.

'It's OK. They're not here for us....are you?' she looked over.

'The children can stay in the house, we just want supplies,' the soldier nodded and smiled.

The Keller parents stood to the side, and Amalie cried out to her mother, 'Mother,' and Jakob yelled to father, 'Papa' as the Luftwaffe unleashed its reign of terror. The Russians retaliated and the Kellers ran for cover.

'Mama!' Amalie screamed. As Leo and Eva ran for cover, the world around them felt like hell on earth. The Luftwaffe flew low and unleashed their hail of death on the unsuspecting Soviets. A fire broke out and clouds of smoke surrounded the Kellers, suffocating them. As soon as the bombs dropped, the world as Amalie had known it became a luminescent fireball. Thick grey ash billowed into the sky, and they became shrouded by a veil of dark smoke. The fire flicked and crackled and crawled up the trunks of the surrounding trees, enveloping them whole. It devoured everything in its path, and its intense heat forced the family outside their home.

'Papa,' Jakob yelled out but to no answer. The painful silence and all the nerves in the children's bodies pleaded for the catastrophe to stop.

'AMALIE, JAKOB, LEO?' Eva cried out and ran towards the children, rushing them inside away from the chaos. Her voice quivered in overwhelming fear as she searched for her husband.

Leo stormed open the door, shoving it closed behind him, and the Luftwaffe disappeared from view. He could feel death swallowing him whole, and he raised a finger to his lips to silence the other members so he could listen for the aircraft to encircle.

CHAPTER 2

"Surviving is the only glory in war."
Samuel Fuller

Amalie wrote to her Grandparents in Britain often, her Nan lived for her granddaughter's letters. She missed the grandchildren dearly, and every day she would wait at the entrance of her home for the postman to bring her another letter. Never did they mention the horrors the Keller children were experiencing, instead Amalie was brief and buoyant. Her grandparents were old and frail, and they needn't know about the atrocities where the Kellers resided. Over the next few days, Amalie started to miss her grandparents; she wrote them the letter in hopes of seeing them once again.

Hi Nana,

I am in the best of health and it's my birthday tomorrow. I wish you were here. For the moment, my lessons have been suspended, there are many changes here. Well, things are moving pretty smoothly, all I do is eat and sleep, if I don't get out soon I will look like a barrel. I'd like to buy a dress for my birthday but every day Mother is crying and I don't know why. I try to comfort her but it doesn't help. Father is sad and says I cannot have the new dress. He says I will have to wait until the war is over. It is very boring here and we're always hungry. When can I see you again?

She never did recall whatever happened to that

letter, and she never did see her Nana again.

Amalie's mother and father came home one evening wearing a badge on their clothing and pinned two more on the coats of their son and daughter. Amalie looked straight into her mother's blue eyes, once bright and ambitious now grey and dead.

'Amalie, come here please, lift your arm.' Leo instructed his daughter to raise her arm so the yellow star could be attached to her clothing. A yellow star with "Jude" ("Jew") inscribed in the centre of the patch. This badge made a distinction; the previous day just a person on the street but now, there were Jews and non-Jews.

'This is ludicrous.' Eva shook her head at Leo whilst she stitched the badge onto the clothing.

'We don't have any choice.' Leo waved a poster he snatched from the wall outside. It read, *"Remember the badge, have you already put on the badge? Before leaving the building, put on the badge!"*

'Everyone is staring, Leo, we can't carry on like this. We're like prisoners in our own home.'

The badge represented more than humiliation, it meant shame. It meant fear. If the Kellers forgot their badge, they faced being fined, imprisoned, or worse. Families had been beaten and put to death as a constant reminder not to forget their badges.

Eva ceased smiling. She became void. Her eyes were dazed, and her confidence disappeared, isolating herself in a room. She became a shadow of her old self. The shine in her eyes never returned, and she gave up. Amalie's friend, Beatrice Muchmann, had said, "Having to wear the yellow star was the moment when deep fear and misery took hold."

By now Amalie was salvaging scrap metal, paper, wasted food, and glass for recycling. Despite the sadness, she played with other children. Bomb sites were tempting play areas, and she found many gems among the rubble, finding shrapnel souvenirs and chippings of broken pottery. The American servicemen were very generous; she remembered one giving her chewing gum and chocolate, something her parents could never afford. She and her brother often ran off to parties held by the servicemen at their bases; one advised Amalie to always have her eyes on the sky.

By June, 1940, small scale bombing raids began on Britain, and so the Battle of Britain began. Concerned for his parents, Mr Keller placed his wife and children in hiding.

'You can't leave us now!' Eva pleaded with her husband.

'Keep your heads low, stay out of trouble. I will be back as soon as I can. But, I just can't leave Ma and Pa on their own.'

'Father,' Amalie cried. Her father bent down to kiss his daughter and cupped her face into his hands.

'Amalie, I'm going to check on Nana and Grandpa. I won't be long.'

Jakob cuddled Amalie close and nodded at his father.

'Take care of the girls for me, Jakob; you're the man of the house while I'm away.'

'Yes, Papa.'

Leo pulled his coat up towards his face and grabbed his case; he left at dusk and returned to

Britain. The Kellers never saw him again.

Many Jews concealed their identity and continued to live with false identification; others hid in attics and shelters. For the Kellers, hiding was a task that took an extraordinary risk. Their mother took them to many shelters, but they were full. The family couldn't stay where they were or they would starve. They were forced closer and closer to the city.

'Please take us,' she cried to the shelter.

'Two children, that is all,' the woman answered.

'I beg you.'

Amalie looked at her mother pleading and tugged at the shelter lady. 'Please, our daddy has already gone.'

'OK fine, but there is not enough food as it is.'

'I won't eat,' her mother answered, relieved.

She cried more this day, hugging the children tightly, wiping their faces and kissing their cheeks.

'Everything will be OK,' she whimpered.

This summer, the Kellers were ordered to report to the nearby city for deportation, but they stayed at the shelter. They slept and prayed, ate bread and shared the water that was given to them by the non-Jewish family that took them in.

The non-Jewish family explained to the Kellers that life dictated by the Nazi Regime was strange for them as well, and that at a moment's notice the Kellers must go into hiding. Hitler's private army would regularly visit the farm, measure the land and they were the ones who dictated what crops would and wouldn't be needed to be grown. They would count their chickens, dictate how many eggs were to be supplied, and if there were any shortfalls on the quota, then the father would need to purchase them from the Black Market.

The families in hiding were sad, and their ears deafened with the bombings above ground. The shelter had been raided before, the dogs sniffed and sniffed, and they waited motionless, frozen in fear for hours on end, living through hours of terror, but this day was different.

The hatch opened, and the man shouted.

'You must go, NOW.'

But it was too late; the police had found their hiding place.

'There you are, little rats,' an SS smiled.

'How could you?' cried the shelter lady to the farmer.

'I had no choice,' he mouthed.

'And you will be rewarded for your loyalty.' The soldier turned to the farmer and flicked him a gold coin. Catching it greedily, the farmer left and the SS pulled the families out from the shelter by their hair. The dogs barked and snarled, their teeth glistening in the moonlight pushing the prisoners closer together like sheep. The screams were loud as a blood-curdling scream could be, and the Kellers were loaded onto transport like cattle.

'What is happening?' Eva cried out to the other families. She was distraught, grabbing at the clothing of the fellow Jews that are pushed and shoved onto the wagons. 'Where are we going?'

'Shush, stay quiet or you will get us all killed.' A woman angrily snarled.

'Get moving,' a uniformed man snapped and pushed the butt of his rifle at the nape of Eva's neck.

'Auschwitz,' whimpered a man huddled in the corner of the wagon from a previous pickup.

The families were loaded and prepared for their journey to Auschwitz-Birkenau; a concentration and extermination camp. Each transport consisted of one thousand people, a mixture of men, women, and children of all different ages all squeezed into wagons like cattle. Jakob spoke loudly among the chaos; he tried to calm the storm.

'Please everyone stay calm.'

'Shut up, little boy.'

'Please! You're frightening the children. Please just sit where you can.'

He tried to calm the terror and sought order by asking that half of the young people stand and the other half sit, taking it in turns to alternate every four hours whilst the older people, women and children, would be permanently seated to make this three-day journey as comfortable as possible. Some of the carts were open-topped, others were closed. A bucket was tossed inside for human waste, and once the last prisoner was loaded, there was a muffled sound of closing bolts. A whistle blew and the train started moving. The doors were shut, leaving them in almost complete darkness, and the grills were closed to prevent escape. A flicker of light and air filtered through the cracks. This was a journey that some didn't survive; and a journey that Amalie would never forget; there was no food, no water and people collapsed from exhaustion.

'My baby is dead, my baby is dead!' one woman shouted hysterically and the Kellers could do nothing to comfort her.

Amalie wanted to jump but God forbid they landed in Germany. The cart remained quiet for most of the journey, a few stops with the soldiers yelling, 'If anyone is missing you will be punished,' whilst pointing the rifle in the prisoner's direction.

The soldiers poked and prodded the prisoners, they laughed among themselves. 'Let's throw them off.'

People wanted to survive; it was a dog-eat-dog time and everyone panicked if someone tried to escape through the small window on the side of the wagon, and Amalie, too, was frightened the SS would shoot if they escaped.

She stayed where she was, her face looking outward from the slats of the wooden wagon. The breeze offered slithers of fresh air that kept the nauseating stench at bay. As the bodies pushed and shoved, tempers rose. Her brother grabbed her pulling her close to his body, and he whispered calmly into her ear.

'I'll protect you, for as long as I shall live.'

By the time they arrived at their destination, four people had already died.

They were shuffled off the wagon into queues staying with their mother and some other two thousand people, and they reached out urgently among the swarm and confusion. Possessions were eagerly snatched away and put to one side, and the people were shoved to the other side.

People were crying, dogs were barking, everyone tried to make sense of this place; a place they never knew existed. The large German Shepherd dogs barked, and their coats were covered in mud. As they growled at the prisoners, their mouths salivated with hunger. Their teeth were sharp and visible as they glared with a wild craze at the frightened people. The dogs' paws scraped at the ground whilst they tugged at the leads. They were monsters.

The children were holding onto their mother for dear life, and prisoners who knew their fate whispered warnings to the newcomers.

'Don't say you're too young, don't say you're ill. Say you are fit and healthy, strong and you want to work and don't say you belong together.'

'Put on my coat, Amalie, so you look bigger,' her mother whispered.

'No Mother, I don't need it.'

'Just do it! Listen to me for once.'

Amalie prepared herself to be older but the SS-man did not ask any questions. A Nazi guard looked at Amalie and hesitated but motioned with a stick. Jakob and Amalie were to be pulled to the left and their mother was pulled to the right. There was no time for goodbyes. Jakob and Amalie were left holding onto each other, Amalie cried for her mother.

'Mother? Where is my mother going?'

At this moment, Amalie hadn't realised it would be the last time she would ever see her mother's face; it would be the last memory of her, screaming as she was dragged away from her children.

A woman standing beside Amalie and Jakob pointed to a smoking chimney. 'There, that is where she's going.'

They were herded into a hall to undress, thankfully away from the sun that burned their skin.

After registration, the children were stripped of clothing and prepared for their hair to be shaved. For the first time, Amalie felt inhuman, stripped of any identity. She looked around and saw many other girls her own age with clippers cutting each other's hair. Tears descend her cheeks as her brown locks fell to the ground.

'Now we all look alike,' a girl said to her. 'Doesn't matter if you are rich or poor, blonde or brown-haired, we will all share the same fate.'

Jakob wore a striped uniform, a size too small, and a striped cap. As the cold metal blade of the scissors touched Amalie's skin she winced and for the first time, she saw her brother cry. But allowing the humiliation of having her head shaved enabled Amalie to pass the first test.

Before dawn, the prisoners were roused from their overcrowded wooden beds for roll call.

It was their early wake-up call. The prisoners were addressed in German, and a girl next to Amalie kindly translated as a new crowd of Jews were escorted into the camp. They queued up alongside Amalie's group and she overheard the conversation.

'*Willkommen in Auschwitz.*'

'He's welcoming us to Auschwitz,' she whispered.

'QUIET! "I am Franz Hössler. I am in charge of the economic function of the camp, and on behalf of the camp administration, I bid you welcome. This is not a holiday resort but a labour camp. Just as our soldiers risk their lives at the front to gain victory for the Third Reich, you will have to work here for the welfare of a new Europe. How you tackle this task is entirely up to you. The chance is there for every one of you. We shall look after your health, and we shall also offer you well-paid work. After the war, we shall assess everyone according to his merits and treat him accordingly. Now, would you please all get undressed? Hang your clothes on the hooks we have provided and please remember your number. When you've had your bath, there will be a bowl of soup and coffee or tea for all. Oh yes, before I forget, after your bath, please have ready your certificates, diplomas, school reports, and any other documents so that we can employ everybody according to his or her training and ability."'

'He says we are in a labour camp, but he's lying to them. Those poor unsuspecting souls have no idea what lies before them in those chambers.'

Amalie laughed explosively full of shock and horror.

'We arrived and saw the smoking chimneys. But, this is a factory isn't it?' Amalie's mouth dropped open as the other prisoners enlightened her to the harsh reality; the smoke that rose was from the crematorium.

'We must warn them!' Amalie pleaded.

'Then you will die, there is nothing we can do for them.'

The entire camp stood in their meagre clothing and was rushed into queues so their names could be called, standing completely still for hours at a time. Come sunshine or rain, orders and instructions were read out as everyone was counted. Jakob stood next to his sister and cupped Amalie's bare scalp, it was all the comfort he could offer. She closed her eyes and folded her arms tightly around herself and she reminded herself of the words:

ARBEIT MACHT FREI
Work sets you free

It had offered Amalie the false hope that hard work would result in her and her brother's freedom.

As many as nearly two thousand prisoners at a time would have to share the toilet facilities, and the smell was eye-watering. It was a concrete block with a hole to sit on. Only in 1944 were sinks and toilets installed in a small area for each block. They had no sanitation or privacy, and men, women, and children would share, having to wash in dirty water. No soap and no change of clothing for months on end. Within a few days, her brother's once small uniform began to hang. After they were counted, they waited patiently, not uttering a word, waiting for their bowl of soup. Amalie was lucky if she found a potato peel, and the accompanying piece of black bread allowed for slightly better digestion of the watery soup.

'Make it last,' an inmate advised, but she was so hungry. Food played a huge role at the camp and was also one of the greatest problems. The rations were merely to keep them alive but not enough for nutrition or energy that they needed. Many died during the night, so she stole their bread they had saved. She mumbled to herself, 'and I'm taking your boots, too.' Every day was taken as it came. She smuggled fruit into her trousers and potatoes she put into her clogs. First, they took the young, then the older ones, then the parents. They wanted to annihilate them. When the children had to report to work, she begged her brother not to go but he had no choice. They knew they had to work, if they worked they were safe because they were profitable. Without work, the prospect of surviving was slim.

'Nothing leaves this house,' a guard spewed. The female SS in charge was the cruellest person Amalie had ever seen. She barked at the prisoners, kicked and pulled at their ears to hurry along and she remembered her name as if it was inscribed on her arm like the tattoo they were given.

One male guard had decided Amalie didn't resemble a Jew; he was much kinder, treated her nicer and gave her food.

As she would fall asleep she would dream, she would dream that she would be reunited with her mother and father and this was all just a horrific nightmare. Amalie woke from the stench, nervous, hysterical and covered in sweat, to the rotting smell of bodies decomposing outside her confinement. The flies circling indicated they had been there for a while but still she had hope, as long as the sun shined it was a new day and as the light beamed onto her face she realised she would survive. She prayed she wouldn't die after her mother, but she couldn't face being alone either.

Sharing the bed with her brother made the impossible just about bearable. With very little to eat and one blanket to share, starvation rations, disease, lice and bed bugs, all that mattered was that they were together and it was what kept her alive. She grabbed her throat and stroked where she could still feel the hands of her father choking her to quell her crying and ironically for a moment she was there again feeling her father's hands around her throat.

CHAPTER 3

"All things truly wicked start from Innocence."
Ernest Hemingway.

'If you want to see the sun go down, you will work until we tell you to stop, little girl.' The SS officer's slimy smile extended from ear to ear.

'Es ist fertig,' *this is finished,* snarled another female authoritarian.

A girl of similar age to Amalie rushed towards her, took her hand, and quietly slipped into the crowd.

'You want to stay well away from that one, Amalie.'

'That's Dr Helga Oppenheimer, she loves children. Rumour has it, once she has you in her clasp there's no escaping. Apparently, she removes your arms and legs while you're awake. Some say she even eats the parts she removes.'

Amalie learned over the following days who she could bribe and who she should avoid. Oppenheimer was feared among the children at the camp; many friends and relatives did not return after visiting her surgery. She conducted some of the most painful medical experiments during her time at Auschwitz, purposely inflicting wounds on live subjects apparently for the greater good, helping simulate combat wounds of her fellow German comrades.

The clanging of metal stopped the prisoners working momentarily; the indication that food was being prepared.

'Move before you're told to do so and you die,' an SS Officer warned. 'You won't get a second warning.'

'Keep your head down, do not answer back, never argue and just do as you are asked.' A girl in her late teens advised.

'I am your Kapo,' a female guard declared. She was to be their new block commander. Her eyes fixated to Amalie's group and she pierced them with her stare.

'Komm her,' *come here*, A girl pushed Amalie forward, volunteering her services and she fell at the Kapo's feet.

'I need a girl, to fetch my food, my cigarettes, and anything else I require.' She grabbed Amalie's chin, yanking her face in the Kapo's direction. 'Du wirst es machen.' *You will do it.*

Amalie couldn't believe her luck.

'She's obviously looking for a Jew,' a prisoner disappointedly commented.

'How can she tell?' Amalie questioned the fellow inmate.

'We're all identified by coloured triangles. Here...' he pointed to his shirt 'is the inverted triangle with lettering to signify our imprisonment. If you are a criminal, yours would be green. A political prisoner wears red, homosexuals are pink and Jehovah Witnesses are purple. They help the guards distinguish from a distance who to assign what tasks to what detainee. For example, those wearing a green badge (a convicted criminal) may be of tough temperament and best suited for Kapo duty.

'What are the black triangles?' Amalie asked.

'Those are given to work-shy inmates. Those are the gipsies, mentally ill, or disabled. Addicts are in that category, you're better off staying away from them, especially as the pretty little thing you are. She knows you're a Jew because you wear the yellow badge. Now you're her bitch.'

Now as a Jewish slave, often Amalie pondered whether to walk in after the hoards of people she guided to their death. She wanted it all to end. But, she had a thirst for life, and she wanted to avenge the death of her mother. Amalie had to help burn bodies, haul coal to fuel the furnace, collect any gold from the inmates' teeth and collect ashes from the crematorium. The crematorium was a huge building, and the ovens ran daily, but at least it offered warmth away from the bitter cold.

By October, 1944, the camp started to evacuate.

'Shall we go?' Jakob suggested.

'Where are they going?' Amalie asked her brother.

'Do you care?'

'Something is wrong.'

The choice was in the prisoners' hands. For once they could decide their fate; stay at the camp or leave.

'Well, what shall we do, Amalie, be evacuated with the others?'

'I can't, I can't leave. I can't leave everyone, they would never make it.' Amalie pointed towards her fellow inmates knowing they were too sick and emaciated to make the journey in the snow. Thousands of prisoners marched the "death march" days before the liberation. Many didn't survive and those who couldn't keep up were shot and left to die. Amalie chose to stay at the camp, Jakob chose to go.

In the early morning hours of the 27th of January, 1945, the Red Army liberated Amalie's camp, but when the Soviets arrived they found ruins of large gas chambers where some one million Jews had been murdered. The Nazis had attempted to hide the evidence of mass genocide but had left just over a thousand survivors who were able to retell the monstrous crimes they had endured. Mounted on ponies, they proceeded with caution fearful of a Nazi ambush but there was no trace of a German in the vicinity.

'THERE!' yelled a Lieutenant as they spotted people half-naked and emaciated standing behind barbed wire.

'Please…' murmured a scrawny man, his hands reaching for the soldiers. Initially wary, the inmates eventually realised who the soldiers were.

'We're alone,' an inmate cried. 'Please help us.'

A fire burned in the distance where "Canada" was located. That's where Amalie had taken the precious belongings of her fellow prisoners, and they burned for days even during the liberation.

It was a day the prisoners feared would never come, a day the tanks arrived and the captives walked out. The prisoners became survivors. The gates opened and the soldiers cried. Amalie hid in the corner of her block, she shivered, terrified, unknowingly realising that this was the day she could leave. A soldier stood in front of her and she screamed. He stood tall and broad. He resembled a bear, and Amalie cowered further into the depths of her bunker.

'It's OK, come on,' he whispered.

As Amalie was guided towards the gate, the soldiers looked at each other in horror.

'What is this place?' they queried.

'Hell if I know,' a soldier shrugged as they tread carefully through the snow.

'There are children here, good grief, and bodies everywhere.'

'It's a slaughterhouse, Lieutenant, nothing less.'

'There are even watch towers for armed guards and machine guns fifty meters apart, death barracks and crematoriums. How many people have died here? There are bones, bones everywhere,' he said in disbelief.

'And piles of shoes and human hair?'

'There must be thousands of corpses?' he answered.

'Just round up as many survivors as you can and offer them blankets, comfort, food, anything; just get them out of here.'

Amalie walked on sore feet towards the sign she had seen at the gate. Work *had* set her free, but she was alone.

'Come on, Amalie,' a girl called, taking her hand. She hugged a soldier tightly around the neck thanking him and scoffed the bread he offered, but Amalie wouldn't eat.

'Come on child, eat.'

But Amalie stared. She didn't speak and she didn't eat, she couldn't help but remember her brother. She knew he was too weak to have made the journey alive, but she couldn't convince him. He tried to keep his promise, he wanted to get help, and he wanted to liberate his sister.

The Soviet soldier grabbed the back of Amalie's head and tried to put the bread between her lips, but she growled and snarled. He looked at his comrades, helpless and tearful.

'She's too far gone Lieutenant,' he sighed with a tear in his eye.

'No, she isn't! Keep trying. She's just an innocent caught up in all this.'

'I'm afraid anything innocent in that one died long ago.'

Celebrations were thin. The Red Army had successfully reached the concentration camps, and Hitler's attempt on the destruction of the Soviet's Red Army was a failure, and limited the implementation of the Hunger Plan. It had, however, managed to starve to death some 3.3 million Soviet prisoners and a vast number of civilians.

Back in 1925, Adolf Hitler declared in his autobiography in the second volume of *Mein Kampf, Chapter 14, Eastern Orientation or Eastern Policy,* that he wanted to invade the Soviet Union, and over the next few years he spoke openly about the idea of gaining territory.

On the 3rd of October, 1941, he announced,

"I have come here today to deliver a short introductory address on the Winter Help Scheme. This time it was particularly difficult for me to come here because in the hours in which I can be here a new, gigantic event is taking place on our Eastern front.

For the last forty-eight hours an operation of gigantic proportions is again in progress, which will help to smash the enemy in the East. I am talking to you on behalf of the millions who are at this moment fighting and want to ask the German people at home to take it upon themselves, in addition to other sacrifices that of Winter Help this year."

Hitler truly believed that the German people needed living space, *Lebensraum,* in the East and it would truly nurture the German people. Although, when he became Chancellor of Germany in 1933, he dismissed it as "fantasies behind bars" whilst he was in jail.

CHAPTER 4

There's a first time for everything.

It was the 30th of January, 1945, and the outcome of World War II was clear. The Führer knew defeat was inevitable, and on his 12th anniversary of his accession to power, he made one last public radio speech.

"I expect every German to do his duty to the last and that he be willing to take upon himself every sacrifice he will be asked to make; I expect every able-bodied German to fight with the complete disregard for his personal safety; I expect the sick and the weak or those otherwise unavailable for military duty to work with their last strength; I expect city dwellers to forge the weapons for this struggle and I expect the farmer to supply the bread for the soldiers and workers of this struggle by imposing restrictions upon himself; I expect all women and girls to continue supporting this struggle with utmost fanaticism."

Hitler warned the German people that after the war the European nations would not be able to withstand bolshevism by the Bolshevik Jews and rise of the Soviets, and all of Germany would crumble.

The war devastated more than just buildings. It had a profound effect on people, especially the children. They were the nation's future, the pillars for a brave new world. Their generation had been jeopardised by the previous.

A ten year old girl was deaf, caused by the bombs unleashed on her village. A seven year old boy was maimed when his wonderful new toy turned out to be a grenade. These and so many others were now without their families and roamed the streets like wolf packs. Without any form of education or support system, they became adults despite their age. They begged, stole, and survived only by their own instincts. These were the children of tomorrow. Would the horrific circumstances of their lives give rise to another Hitler?

Much of Germany was dead, and life in Germany was broken. People were left wandering looking for food, each other, and their homes. Notice boards would read, "*Ich suche meine Frau"* or *"Ich suche nach meiner Familie*." Half of the population were looking for *someone.* The people were stunned by what had hit them; a war that they had encouraged, a war they started. A nation of civilised, sophisticated people brainwashed into following such a malevolent dictator that the world had ever seen.

Amalie, barefoot and riddled with lice, had survived the hunger, the cold, and loss of identity. She latched onto the older girl who helped her out of the camp, and together they were sent to a town where they were promised food, and hopefully, a new home. They passed through villages and some sympathetic residents offered buckets of soup at their front doors, but everyone was fearful and afraid.

The towns had been destroyed, for Hitler wanted total destruction. In his eyes, Germany had failed him, and they deserved to die when he died.

The once prosperous villages where all the women

were sent to concentration camps and all the men were shot and buried in one common grave were now desolate and in ruins. The children were sold to various families, now lost forever. The effects after the war lingered for years from the hands of the SS and other Nazi followers, and place and time meant nothing; links between people had been destroyed as well.

Villages now resembled ruins, and hunger twisted the country into an economic cripple that would last for decades. Humans were reduced to living like animals. And nothing reduces a population like a plague. The country had hit rock bottom. It needed revival, but revival with rats, epidemic and disease, lice and famine? Revival achieved through hunger? People left scavenging through rubbish bins for scraps of food like mere wild dogs? A starved nation was not a sturdy nation and therefore revival meant death, reducing the mass population through hunger.

"We Germans must number twice the population of our neighbours. Therefore we shall be compelled to destroy one-third of the population of all adjacent territories. We can best achieve this through systematic malnutrition – in the end far superior to machine guns. Starvation works more effectively especially among the young." Wrote Field-Marshal von Rundstedt.

Of all the victims of WW2, the most pitiful and sorrowful were the most precious; the future – the children. Even after liberation, they were heirs to fear, hunger, and hate. Their destiny was to be nourished in a world of desperation and despair, fertilising the ground with seeds for WW3. Yet, in the search for food, a life force began to stir. The younger children were taken in by families, but, for the older children such as Amalie, they had to find their own way and survive in the woods.

People that sauntered through trees that hadn't been stripped by shrapnel and whose gardens shed no sign of burn and whose crops were unaffected by blasts could never imagine the horrors that were endured. Screaming children only signified children at play at nearby schools, and shop shortages only meant temporary discomfort, *not* death. No matter how vivid the imagination, it just cannot convey the full meaning of what others had undergone. But, geographical differences were no bar to devastation, and justice had given the warning to all; people that do not understand history are doomed to repeat it.

The world post WW2 just cannot survive another war. In an effort to unite and end war forever, the United Nations looked to the first organisation it created; the UNRRA (*United Nations Relief and Rehabilitation Administration*). The outpouring of each nation to each war-stricken friend and neighbour provided the basis for peace, and soon other private relief and welfare organisations blended their efforts with contributions from their governments.

The emergency items were required by all and served as the common ground among the people for unity. As every savaged, tired, yet liberated area fought to regain control, strength, and vigour, the people united. A welfare specialist from Australia, a doctor from Cuba, a nurse from Belgium, a child expert from England, a therapeutic from Ohio, all aid from Canada, Norway and many other nations... all operated together despite the disadvantage of language barriers. They all learned constructive, invaluable lessons in international teamwork. People were taught occupations so the men could stand on their own two feet again, and everyone learned to share to survive. Homes were remade, the farmers continued despite warnings of mines, and once again smoke rose from chimneys of family homes. UNRRA reported progress, albeit straining and exhausting, all for the very future of the people; for in the words of Thomas Payne, *"If there be trouble, let it be in my time that my child may have peace."*

If fear was created among the people and the young, then what would sprout from these seeds? Would the youth from these ravaged lands become new Führers or lovers of liberation?

"It would be a dangerous error to think of the Holocaust as simply the result of the insanity of a group of criminal Nazis. On the contrary, the Holocaust was the culmination of millennia of hatred; scapegoating and discrimination targeting the Jews, what we now call anti-Semitism". UN Secretary-General António Guterres.

CHAPTER 5

I got a taste for blood when I was licking my own wounds.

Amalie had become like many others; an orphan. She relied on her fading memories to survive, and later travelled with other children to East Germany where she was placed in an orphanage; there was nothing here.

The orphanage was an immense grey Victorian styled home, and as the front door opened, Amalie was greeted by the stench; fear, boiled vegetables, and urine. The orphanage was located in a remote rural location of eastern Germany, and the children inside peeked at the newcomer at the front door.

'Welcome, and who might this be?' The woman leant down to look at Amalie, but Amalie remained quiet and she hid behind the arm of her guardian despite the woman appearing sweet, motherly, and affectionate.

'She's a quiet one,' Amalie's guardian answered, clutching her close.

'We have near to one hundred children here, and every one of them has their special requirements. I'm sure she will fit right in.' The lady of the orphanage waved Amalie inside and she pointed to where she could wait. Amalie sat on the couch by the hallway. Her temporary guardian and the lady of the orphanage continued their discussions whilst perusing the grand building. 'Our children have many problems and are in terrible condition, but can you blame them?' Several children looked at the newcomers on the verge of tears.

'I can only try to imagine what they have seen,' Amalie's guardian answered as they disappeared and Amalie got up to explore. The children whispered and giggled and hurried to their rooms. The floors were immaculate, brand new linen was on the beds, and not a cobweb could be found, but the overwhelming smell was nauseating. Amalie ventured around, walking past the children, and walked into the bathrooms, each covered with excrement. The water had been cut off, and none of the toilet facilities were working. She closed in on her guardian and tugged at her sleeve to turn her attention to the inside of the bathrooms.

'What is it, Amalie?' she smiled.

'Oh, the water has been cut off I'm afraid, but we have a latrine outside,' the lady stated.

'But, it's minus twenty degrees out there!' the guardian exclaimed.

'There isn't much else I can do. We're doing the best we can.'

The kitchen was the next stop; meat was a rarity but today was a special occasion. The orphanage was receiving many new guests, and the local people had kindly donated food to help with the influx of post-war children. A cook rushed around hurriedly and dropped meat onto the floor; he looked up, hesitated, but threw it back into the pot.

'Come here, Caleb. Say hello to Amalie.' The little boy ran away, clearly terrified. The tour finalised by the bedrooms.

'This will be Amalie's room,' the lady stated whilst gesturing with her hand.

Ten beds adorned one of the bedrooms. They were perfectly made, uniform, nothing personal, no personal belongings; ready for one child to leave and another to arrive. Amalie was guided to a bed in the corner; an unopened toothbrush, toothpaste, and a small bar of soap sat on her pillow.

'How many members of staff are there?' her guardian asked.

'We have four members of staff. Each takes it in turns to work around the clock.' She said it like she was proud that so few staff could tender that many children.

The building had lost its grand splendour. A mansion it must have once been, but all that remained was a mansion that once had shone under the sun and was now chipped, broken, dark, and beyond repair.

The scratch marks on the walls were like those of a rabid animal that tried to claw its way out, the windows were broken, and old broken dolls lay on the floor with heads torn away from their bodies. The walls had lost their colour, every step creaked through the shadow-filled hallways, and the children whispered cruel words.

'Amalie, you're no different than the rest of us…just another with no family.'

Amalie slapped the girl.

'Ah...!!' she screamed, holding the side of her face.

'AMALIE – OFFICE NOW.' Amalie was seated in front of the Matron, not the woman that had given her and her guardian the guided tour just days before.

This woman terrorised children with harsh disciplinary methods, and things went from bad to worse as thoughts began to manifest inside Amalie's mind about inflicting physical pain on the bitch that thought of herself as nothing less than a Kapo back at Auschwitz. Amalie viewed her as no different than the Nazi nurses and their Nazi programs, believing they were doing good by following orders, helping out, or fighting for a cause they believed in. The Matron was a large, red-faced woman with a sharp voice and permanent glare. She had a smell like some foul combination of vegetable soup and old shoes, and her black, piercing, beady eyes never stopped looking for the opportunity to correct.

Fear funnelled through the orphanage. Children every day were sent to the Matron's office for scrutinising and punishment for wrongdoings. Many children talked after hours about their brothers and sisters during the war that were sent to nurses who used light rays, formed under the program *Lebensborn,* in an attempt to lighten their hair to the colour of "Super Race Children."

'You're making that up,' one boy dismissed.

'It's true!' another orphan remarked.

'What if we're sent away?'

'The war has finished, we're safe now.'

'With her?' *(The Matron)*

Amalie didn't know what to say, she had no answers. An older girl in her late teens poked at Amalie, '*You* came from the concentration camp. You didn't measure up cosmetically,' she sniggered.

Amalie grabbed the girl's finger and bent it so far back it cracked.

'You crazy bitch!' she screamed.

'Shush, you will wake the wicked witch,' a boy cautioned.

'But…' the older girl cried.

'I didn't see anything,' he winked at Amalie.

The oldest of the group sat on the edge of Amalie's bed.

'Just ignore Patricia. For the record, Pat, in the program *Lebensborn,* thousands of Aryan looking kids were kidnapped from occupied territories and transported to Lebensborn clinics to be indoctrinated as pure Germans. If you refused you were beaten and sent to concentration camps – *lord knows what happened there!*

'And the ones that complied?'

'It's said the *Schutzstaffel* (SS) adopted them, that's why Walter's here.' He pointed at another shy boy sitting on his own.

Walter was a child from the Lebensborn program; he had no family ties and suffered from growing up realising his father was a war criminal. The orphanage offered him shelter in hopes that one day someone might recognise him, instead of him having to live a life shamed with having a German father.

CHAPTER 6

Fools rush in.

'You're not welcome here anymore, Amalie,' Patricia spewed.

By now Amalie was a teenager. She was desperate, and on top of everything else she had lost her father, her mother, and her brother in the death march the day before the liberation of Auschwitz. She learned later that her brother must have marched at night in lines across as officers shot those too ill and exhausted to carry on. She only prayed he took shelter in the woods or some abandoned barn and they soon would be reunited. But, as the days moved on, the prospect of seeing Jakob again drew slim.

Even with her freedom, Amalie had no parents, no possessions, and no place could she call home. Millions upon millions of displaced children swept throughout the country, many sharing her predicament.

Coordinating with their allies, the UNRRA assisted refugees that were driven from their homes by force or necessity and sent workers to offer assistance to care for those in displaced populations.

Amalie hoped and prayed every night someone, somewhere, would find her.

'What are you writing there, Amalie?'

'That's none of your business, Patricia.'

'Well, you won't be here much longer.'

'Don't listen to Pat, Amalie. You're welcome here

for as long as you need,' the nice boy reassured her.

Many children arrived at the orphanage, either on their own, or like Amalie, with a UNRRA team worker. And, like Amalie, many would arrive malnourished and starving, screaming at the smell of food that drifted through the air from the kitchen. Teenagers arrived daily, conditioned to be pro-nationalist and to hate Jews, and within hours, Jews arrived hoping a parent had survived and was actively seeking their child.

Amalie watched as children arrived and grabbed food like animals, but the UNRRA offered lessons in etiquette.

'There's plenty to go around, calm down,' they would say, but the smaller children grabbed slices of bread and scurried off to their rooms to bury it beneath their pillows.

As challenging as it was, the UNRRA created a case file for every child at the orphanage, complete with accompanying photographs and letters, to help reunite orphans with distant family members around the globe. For Amalie, her file quickly filled, she clung to the idea that one day her family would find her and her brother would keep his promise.

However, the younger children didn't know their names and their ages could neither be identified.

'Come, quickly, now, I'd like you to stand still. I'm going to take your photograph,' the care worker smiled as he held the camera in front of the children. The headshots were face on, each child tried to smile with sad eyes staring back at him. They projected the hope that, if their families were still alive they would be alerted to their children's whereabouts, recognise the photo and would rush to pick them up. In most cases for the German children, it happened. But a dark fear grew as each Jewish child had their photo taken that from this point onwards, they were alone in the world. Many children were traumatised so badly, they had forgotten who they were, their names, ages, or even where they came from; and other children like Amalie believed their own lies that they had to tell to survive roll call at labour camps.

'Nobody wants you, Amalie. It's been weeks and no one has come to collect you,' Patricia sniggered.

Amalie didn't tell her she knew of her family ties; that Patricia was the daughter of a German commandant at Auschwitz.

'And you, Patricia, who is coming for you?'

Amalie humoured her.

'Well,' she smiled, 'Father's sister in Leipzig is coming next week.'

Patricia was proud of her father and extremely fanatical in her support for the Third Reich. It didn't grant her many friends at the orphanage, and her infatuation for pushing anti-Semitism angered other children. Patricia had grown into a bitter, disillusioned young woman who knew the result of exploitation and greed and grew uninterested in uniting and going against everything she was taught.

Nobody really wanted the children; they didn't want to believe the stories the children told. And as the world's countries rapidly filled their refugee quotas, the world became closed and refugees were left questioning, *"Where do we go?"*

Thousands of children grew up in silence. No bedtime stories, no hugs and kisses, no reassurance from mother and father within a loving family, nothing. At night, the ward was silent and the younger children learned not to cry because why cry if there is no one to comfort them? They were ignored, forgotten, out of sight, out of mind.

By now, Amalie had been at the orphanage a few weeks and children came and went so the arrival of a blonde-haired, blue-eyed girl came as nothing of a surprise.

'She came here last night,' stated the young orphanage worker. 'A good looking child like her will find a home in no time.'

'Where was she found?' another worker asked.

'They found her lying in the street. Walked some distance I'd say. Her shoes are worn through and her feet are blistered, where she came from or where she was heading to, lord knows!'

The orphanage's medic examined the young girl; the half-starved girl of no older than six years. Her somewhat diminutive stature and pale face were as cute as a button, and Amalie knew she wouldn't be here long.

As the weeks continued, the young girl was just one among many that had arrived at the orphanage, just another victim of the systematic abuse to be inflicted by the power-crazed haughty sadist – The Matron.

Yet, as Amalie had envisioned, a couple arrived, having lost their own child, and took the little girl before she was flogged, confined in solitary for days, kicked, and cursed upon. The orphanage was hated, and people did everything they could to avoid ending up there, but those that had no choice were vulnerable or brazen. The orphanage represented everything the Nazis would have liked to have liquidated; the young, the infirm, or people physically deformed or mentally handicapped. Amalie appreciated the help from the UNRRA but couldn't help believe that the residents of the orphanage deserved better.

'The UNRRA has made another delivery,' the kind boy excitedly stated as he looked out the dirty cracked window.

'Oh good,' Patricia said, 'enough of this rubbish.'

That *rubbish* that Patricia referred to was merely food a few days old; food that Amalie certainly wouldn't turn her nose up at. A bit of mould on her bread was the least of her worries at Auschwitz.

'Patricia, "No one is more insufferable than he who lacks basic courtesy",' Amalie smiled.

'Oh do shut up, Amalie,' Patricia answered.

Keller learned at the orphanage that she was growing into a woman of opportunity. The opportunity lay everywhere, and as long as the sun rose, there was a chance of something beautiful happening; whether it was taunting the egotistical Patricia or taking solace in reading. Given her nature, Amalie operated covertly through the orphanage and often caused consternation among the other children.

While she sat in the dining room during mealtime, the ever so tiresome Patricia seated beside her once again.

'Don't eat it all, Amalie, we wouldn't want you getting fat now,' she taunted. 'Let me take this piece of bread and save you the trouble.' Patricia reached towards Amalie's plate, and Amalie picked up her fork and drove it home into Patricia's hand. Patricia screeched a blood-curdling scream, reaching to grab the fork but Amalie held it firmly.

'If there is anything that I loathe more than your face, it's discourtesy, and that is unspeakably ugly to me. You're a pig, Patricia; the free-range kind, and one day you will be someone's bacon. So please, if you would, take this piece of bread to Helga. As you said, I'm trying to watch my figure.'

Later that evening, Amalie and Patricia glared at one another from across the bedroom. The heavy footsteps indicated the beast was on her way. The children threw their heads into their pillows and threw the quilt over their bodies. But Amalie remained upright.

'KELLER!'

The matron stood at the entrance to the bedroom calling Amalie's name. The children jumped and bolted upright glaring at the doorway.

'KELLLLLER!' she screamed. Amalie crawled out of bed and walked towards the large woman. Her unforgiving bun pulled her face so taught it made her a harsh, psychopathic, and cruel educator. The matron was a power-crazed, abusive sadist, and the children quivered when she spoke.

'Yes?' Amalie answered unsympathetically.

'You have a letter.' She dropped the letter on the floor before Amalie could take it and swivelled in her bottle green trouser suit to walk away.

'Cock sucker.' Amalie snarled.

The children began tapping the tables and chanting, 'Ke...ller, Ke...ller,' and the Matron paused. She turned, lowering herself to stare at Amalie.

'Hmmm, you're a lucky little maggot. What fun I

would have with you if you were staying with us.'

Amalie was ready for punishment but it never came. The matron turned and walked away, and Amalie looked into her hands to open the white envelope.

Amalie Keller was one of the lucky ones. She read the first line of a letter that had been in answer to Amalie's photograph. A tear dripped onto the paper when she learned of the death of her grandparents. Amalie's letters were found when her uncle cleared out their home. Yes, Amalie had family after all.

CHAPTER 7

Patience is a killer

After the war, the country saw a surge in new books, and the UNRRA regularly brought round a few for the children in the orphanage. Pre-war libraries had been limited and were full of outdated books covered in layers of dust, but attention to the public libraries became important for the re-education of the people. The Second World War put a hold on public library service, and many books were destroyed. The care workers brought round to the orphanage what they could salvage.

Among the books delivered was a tan one with the design and lettering in black. The spine's edges were gently rubbed, and on the front cover it read *The Mysterious Affair at Styles* by *Agatha Christie.* Amalie couldn't believe her luck; the name *Agatha Christie* had been a favourite author of Amalie's mother. Whilst Amalie was young she would often steal her mother's book to read chapters of *The Secret Adversary*, about a young couple, in love, broke, and looking for excitement. The pair embarked on a daring scheme where they would, "do anything, or go anywhere".

Amalie reminisced about her childhood and how much her life had changed as she scurried off to her room and lay upon the covers of her bed opening the pages with eagerness.

Between the pages of *The Mysterious Affair at*

Styles, she learned that Strychnine is a highly toxic, colourless, and bitter substance, very effective in eliminating vermin; *such as* Patricia. Amalie had remembered seeing the yellowed jar in the kitchen and knew that the day she was to leave from the orphanage, she would slip the Strychnine into Patricia's cold medicine on her bedside table. Amalie didn't fear that the poison would affect any of the children; Patricia was possessive over every aspect of her life including her medicine.

As Patricia's neck and face became stiff, her arms and legs began to spasm and she arched her body placing her head and feet onto the floor. Amalie grabbed her small case with her few belongings and headed for the door.

'You did this to me you bitch!' She frothed at the mouth and even in her last precious moments Patricia couldn't help but have the last word. Amalie turned around to wish Patricia goodbye and smiled.

'*"It is one thing to know that a man is guilty, it is quite another matter to prove him so."*'

As the door closed behind her, Amalie headed for the train station to begin her travel to the address in the letter. A letter only she had read.

Amalie had been given strict instructions in the letter from her uncle, an uncle she had never met. Her journey would be long and chaotic, and Amalie would be among several hundred children that had been accepted into the UK by the Central British Fund, the same organisation that had brought around 10,000 children to Britain just months before the war broke out.

She had heard "England was like the golden land,"

a statement that was supposedly said by a boy named
Izak Perlmutter who had flown to Ascot in 1945.

   She boarded her train as instructed and headed for
Holland, where she departed for the British port of
Harwich. From there, she caught a train to Liverpool
Street Station in London. A driver was waiting and
took her to her new home in Surrey.

III

SURREY, ENGLAND

CHAPTER 8

"The curves of your lips rewrite history."
Oscar Wilde.

England was the chance for a new start, and 1949 saw England surviving the misery of the depression and the Second World War. The bespoke wrought iron gates at her uncle's stately home opened automatically, the grass smelled freshly cut, and the morning dew frozen on the blades sparkled like glass jewels. The flowers were bright and colourful and Amalie's head turned from side to side to take in the scenery. The walls of the home had an imposing air of sandstone solidity, worthy of the impression that grew upwards from the mowed lawn into an ostentatious spectacle. As she drew closer, she held her breath as she took in its magnificence. A man appeared at the front door to greet Amalie.

'You must be Amalie?' the aristocrat asked.

'What gave it away?' she cautiously answered.

'You're the image of your photograph; a little older, the hair a little shorter but, just like your father. Come, come inside.' He gestured whilst wrapping his arm around Amalie's shoulders and took her small case from her.

As Amalie walked through the front door, she was confronted by a soaring ceiling and vast marble flooring. Haunting corridors led in various directions with an elegant flight of stairs before her, and she looked at the stranger for guidance.

'Amalie, this is your home now,' he smiled.

Amalie was fascinated at the Jacobean furnishings. The raw oak reminded her dearly of her father. The historical mementoes and the collection of more than five thousand books pleased Amalie immensely. Family portraits adorned the walls. Amalie recognised her father in one and began stroking it softly.

'Excuse me......' she asked.

'You may call me William, or Uncle William, whichever you find most comfortable.'

'This is my father isn't it?'

'Yes, it is.'

'Where is he?' Amalie questioned.

'Let us go and sit in the drawing-room.' The drawing-room was warm, with a beautifully ornate ceiling, oil paintings on every wall, Persian carpets and a crystal chandelier.

'The art is stunning.' Amalie's eyes wandered from painting to painting and she analysed one up close.

'That one, Amalie, was a gift from our Prime Minister.'

'Churchill?'

'Yes, you wouldn't know as he rarely signed his paintings, but if you look here,' William pointed to a small scribble in the corner, 'you will see his initials. Churchill, if he remembers, only ever adds his initials when he is about to give a painting away, but often they are signed by his frame maker using a brass template.'

'It's beautiful. I had no idea he painted!'

'Yes, in his book *Painting as a Pastime,* he said

that, "painting came to my rescue in a most trying time,".'

'I wish I could paint.'

'You have to start somewhere. Churchill picked up a brush only after a suggestion by his sister-in-law, also a painter. He claimed that at the beginning he was intimidated by the blank canvas, and he diffidently placed a blue daub of paint on its surface to begin the sky and was soon interrupted by the arrival of another painter who promptly grabbed the brush and said "what are you hesitating about?" She took that brush and swept it across the canvas with large ferocious blue strokes, and with that Churchill wrote, "I seized the largest brush and fell upon my victim with berserk fury. I have never felt any awe of a canvas since".'

Amalie burst with laughter.

'You see, dear Amalie, you mustn't allow anything to intimidate you.'

'And, this one?' She pointed to another painting.

'That is your ancestor and his wife, sometime in 1700.' The painting depicted a couple who recently returned from their honeymoon. The figures were placed asymmetrically on the canvas to show that the landscape had become of equal importance to the figures. It showed idealised parkland, winding water and distant hills; the estate of Amalie's lineage.

The woman's bodice was boldly decorated with three large contrasting bows that matched her underdress in the artist's portrait. She appeared to have her sheer apron caught in her left arm and wore a robe *à l'anglaise* or a close-bodied gown; women's fashion of the 18th century. Her newly wedded husband leaned elegantly against a tree stump that was entwined with honeysuckle. His wife, wearing her formal pink and green dress, sat on a fallen tree and looked adoringly into his eyes.

Amalie sat on the edge of the oversized chair, her hands inside her thighs, eager for information.

'Tell me about him, my father.'

'All I know is that soon after his arrival, he headed towards London. With all the bombings by the Luftwaffe, it is doubtful anyone survived. It has been five years now, and I still wait for his return.'

'I miss him.'

'We all do darling. Go upstairs and wash your hands. Dinner will be ready shortly.'

Days with her uncle passed at a phenomenal rate. Never was Amalie bored. Her uncle enlisted the family's stylist to dress and style Amalie, elocution lessons were booked three times a week, flower arranging and cookery classes also became part of daily life. However, Amalie's favourite time was spent watching her uncle play the piano. After waking one morning to the soothing melodies, where every note was weaved with such beauty, Amalie was transfixed. She hurried down the elegant spiral staircase to investigate. She swirled and pirouetted, searching in every room for the source. The heavenly notes were slow yet mesmerising, and her heart beat faster as the sound grew louder and louder, the vibrations causing the hairs on her arms to rise and a spine chilling sensation descended her back.

'Amalie, you frightened me.'

'What was that? That sound?'

'Ah, that was Chopin's *"Spring Waltz."* Did you

enjoy it?'

'Very much... Please play more.'

'After tea, I will show you.'

Amalie became a fast learner; the elocution lessons improved Amalie's spoken accuracy, although she called it *Electrocution* lessons. Amalie was reprimanded most days, and the tutor manhandled the shambolic girl, yet with one word to her uncle, the tutor was fired. It was Amalie's first recognition of how easily she could manipulate men and how men could be so easily succumbed under her whim.

Amalie began to become a lady the day she arrived. In a very short time, her deportment tutor had her walking up and down the corridor with a book on her head, much to her uncle's amusement.

'Why do I have to do this, Uncle?'

'We're going to help your posture. You'll be bent over like an old granny before you are twenty-five if we do not sort it out now,' he laughed. Amalie pursed her lips and laughed. 'Oh Amalie, you are a picture.'

'A picture of what?'

'Never you mind.'

Amalie had been fast-tracked into a lifestyle of haute cuisine and delicate social intercourse. Her uncle had explained to her that becoming a lady was empowering and the benefits were numerous. It displayed self-respect, class, and etiquette; it had nothing to do with wealth.

'We will be hosting an event this evening. I'd be delighted if you helped Mrs Campbell in the kitchen.'

'But I've never cooked.'

As the words left Amalie's mouth, Mrs Campbell entered through the back door to the kitchen carrying a hessian sack. It slumped onto the kitchen side, and Amalie's eyes widened with curiosity. It was time for Amalie to face the reality of country life, and testing her nerve was Mrs Campbell. At least half of a country lady's life would be spent outdoors, hunting, shooting, learning the equipment and the animals, how they're fed, and the aftermath of that with no flinching.

'Don't tell me you're squeamish, dear?'

'Of what?' Amalie pursed her lips.

Mrs Campbell reached inside the sack and withdrew various species of dead bird whilst passing Amalie the menu for this evening that read;

Potages

Consommé à la Monaco Crème Argenteuil

Entrée

Engastrated Fowl stuffed with sausage and cranberry stuffing
Roasted parsnip, cabbage and sautéed potatoes

Grand Marnier Soufflés with Crème Anglaise

~

Learning the social etiquette of fine dining is probably the ultimate indication of one's social standing. It's learning how to behave, how to eat, and how to be a gracious hostess.

Amalie took the menu card and inspected the

courses. *"Engastrated fowl?"* This sounds like a disease.

'What the fuck is that?'Amalie muttered under her breath.

'We do not condone swearing in this house, young Amalie,' Mrs Campbell stated and she shook her head in shame.

'I didn't swear, Mrs Campbell. I said what type of duck is that?'

'Oh, I do apologise. This is called an Aylesbury duck, a good heavy bird,' she smiled and slapped the breast of the animal. Amalie had no idea what an Aylesbury duck looked like but it proved an easy escape from being caught cursing in front of Mrs Rosemary Campbell - the manor's cook.

'Pick it up and hang it on this hook, like this.' Mrs Campbell took one of the limp birds and knocked it onto a hook and proceeded to pluck. Amalie had never seen a bird plucked before.

'Now take the knife and brush it flat against the back of your fingers, tip the knife and slice.'

'I'm not sure how this is learning how to be a Lady, Mrs Campbell.' Amalie's eyebrows creased and she sliced into the meat.

'I will not allow you to be a mockery of this house, Amalie. Your uncle is a kind and generous man.'

'I find it unnecessary.'

'If learning self-respect, manners, and morals are unnecessary, then call me unnecessary as much you wish.'

After a morning of cooking, Amalie was ready to throw in the tea towel. Time had come for drastic change, and the art of learning social intercourse had proven harder than she had thought.

'You're a rough diamond, Amalie, and you need polishing.'

'Mrs Campbell...'

'Yes, dear?'

'What is castrated fowl?' Amalie queried.

'Do you mean engrastrated?'

'Yes, sorry.'

'The art of food in food. I like to think of it as stunt dining, designed to be so outrageous that our guests will be impressed with the trouble we have taken on their behalf.'

'It looks horrible.'

'Darling, people have been stuffing animals into animals since Roman times. Did you know they had a recipe involving a cow, a pig, a goose, a duck and a chicken?'

'With a little gherkin, I hope? There's nothing nicer than a little gherkin. Love it, love it.' Amalie laughed at her posh accent.

'This dish is fundamentally based on skill. Why? Because humans by nature are ridiculously and relentlessly creative, we'll just do crazy things. Tonight I call this dish a *Turducken* – Turkey, duck and chicken. I'm almost positively sure your uncle will be amazed at my creation, he admires one's creativity, and in these dishes we transcend nature either by transforming food or preparing them in a more artistic form. I thus become the painter who adds symbolism to my depiction of nature.'

'It sounds more malicious than delicious if you ask me! Why is meat hung?' Amalie queried.

'Well, they say that it improves the flavour and

allows the enzymes to break down the tissue through dry-ageing and gives the water in the meat chance to evaporate, concentrating the flavour. Give me a piece of twenty-eight day aged beef any day, but thirty-five days of dry ageing, well, that's just royalty. Just add a béarnaise sauce and there you have it: perfection.

'So life really does imitate art.'

'How so, Amalie?'

'Well, I was reading this book...'

'Aha...' Mrs Campbell nodded while plucking feathers from the hanging bird.

'There was this man in eighteenth century France who had such a fertile imagination that he flooded the world with his monstrosities, and his books became a portrayal of everything forbidden in his *then* society. Surrealist artists had such an interest in the Marquis de Sade that the first Manifesto of Surrealism stated that "Sade is surrealist in sadism". Guillaume Apollinaire even said that Sade was "the freest spirit that had ever lived".

'I wouldn't read too much into that, Amalie. He was a twisted, debauched lunatic. Where did you find that out anyway?'

'Uncle's library.'

'Good Lord! I may have to have a quiet word with your uncle about his choice of blasphemous books.'

'It's really hard to imagine anyone getting off on his works, Mrs Campbell.'

'I beg your pardon?'

'Well, he gave prostitutes pills to make them pass wind, and then he would crouch expectantly under their buttocks,' Amalie shrugged.

Mrs Campbell was speechless and wanted to laugh

but knew that would only encourage the young Amalie. 'Can you not find a nice story to read?'

'Oh, but Mrs Campbell, his life's story is so fascinating! He had two daring prison breaks and such a dynamic relationship with a police inspector who hounded him with a diligent obsession and in one of his major scandals, Sade procured the services of a woman, a woman named Rose Keller! How strange is that?'

'Yes very. Now before I lock you up, run along and don't forget to wash your hands.'

CHAPTER 9

If at first, I don't succeed…

Amalie had been drilled in the traditional ruling classes; she learned good deportment, respect and manners. Her unruly behaviour was not tolerated, and she learned how to refine her skills in social and domestic arts. It was a painful process, and at no point along the journey did she forget the haunting memories in her nightmares: the expressions on the faces of the children whose bodies turned to smoke against the vast blue sky. No amount of affluence, prestige, or power could make her forget and neither forgive.

'Amalie,' her uncle told her, 'You must move on. It will eat you up and devour your soul if you allow this terrible act to rule your life. You have the whole world in front of you.'

'Our heads were shaved, and we sat there and didn't know if it would be water or gas. It was water. In the room, they took everything away from us but they couldn't remove my integrity. That I managed to maintain.'

'Amalie…'

'NO, they couldn't take my soul.'

'Amalie, please, leave it be.'

The evening arrived, and Amalie dreaded the whole noble scene. Attending an upper-class twit party of some kind was far from her idea of an evening well spent. She hated the dress, was stupefied with the chit-chat, and looked towards Mrs Rosemary Campbell with open disdain at being forced to flatter the more influential and powerful, yet insipid, guests. It didn't matter that Amalie wore a beautiful dress and her porcelain features were plucked and pruned to perfection, she was still that little girl with a muddy face looking up at her superiors with fear and animosity.

'I need a drink.' William looked at Amalie with total contempt. The last thing he wanted was a wayward alcoholic, 'H2O,' she answered, 'shaken, not stirred.'

'So this is she, the guest of honour?' a pompous gentleman queried.

'Yes,' Amalie's uncle answered, embracing Amalie and squeezing her arm tightly. 'I will be back shortly,' he finalised, kissing her forehead.

'Please don't leave me. I've got mad hair, I can't breathe and I'm wearing scary knickers.'

'You'll be fine.'

'You can't leave me with some of the UK's most dangerous perverts disguised as guests of honour!' Amalie exhaled and William smiled whispering, 'Play nice.'

'We've heard all about you,' the guest said while his eyebrows rose up and down.

'I sincerely hope not.'

'There must be more to know?' he asked. 'You're not quite what I was expecting.'

'I'm sorry to disappoint.'

'Oh no, quite the contrary,' he smiled sliding his finger down the side of Amalie's face to sweep a stray hair aside.

'Do you mind?'

'Not at all,' he smiled.

'Good, then fuck off.'

'Excuse me?' His expression turned from infatuation to horror.

'I don't sugar-coat anything. I'm not a bakery, and neither am I a candy shop.'

Amalie's uncle returned, and the upper-class twit left.

'Was everything all right? I'm sorry I left. Why did *he* leave to quickly?'

'I have no idea, Uncle. Everything was going so smoothly.'

'Your father would have been proud of you tonight. I only wished he was here to see you. Look at you, you're gorgeous.' Amalie's uncle twirled her on the dance floor, the piano music once again erupted, and the room spun to the best of Bach.

'Mrs Campbell, please bring out another bowl of punch.'

'Certainly, Sir,' she nodded.

'Sir William,' the impudent guest returned, 'we thank you so much for your hospitality,' he looked at Amalie with contempt, 'but I'm not quite feeling myself.' Unbeknownst to him, Amalie had laced his last glass of punch with Belladonna, but just enough to cause his heart rate to rise with profuse sweating.

'Are you all right?' Her uncle questioned. The guest glared at Amalie, and she smiled her best bona fide smile for the sake of her uncle and continued to waltz to the music.

CHAPTER 10

"The only way to get rid of temptation is to yield it." Oscar Wilde.

Britain began the 1950s in austerity. It went through huge changes as did Amalie's uncle. Amalie and her uncle were one of the first families to receive television and in doing so, he adopted a new look.

'What do you think?' Amalie laughed at her uncle. At the front of his hair, a quiff, at the back it was swept back like a duck's arse. Amalie's uncle felt like a new man with the much younger Amalie around and tried to keep up appearances, much to her amusement.

Amalie was taught how to be a lady. Dinner table etiquette was new to Amalie, and conversations on topical matters were unknown territory. She soon metamorphosed from a ragged wild child into a fine mannered, genteel woman.

In outside society, Amalie was every inch of a demure lady, but inside the Manor she was adventurous. She had an allure, she was showered with gifts but she wanted more.

The 1950s were a decade of stark contradiction. People often turned to God and blamed Satan for all the evilness in the world, and a new brand of a psychopath was reflected in the eyes of the beautiful housewife with her hair rolled up into tight curls, her red lips and high heels.

Winning the war created euphoria among the people despite not seeing the back of rationing until 1958, and with women now entering the workforce in ever increasing numbers, families found they had disposable income. Pulling together, people rebuilt the country and were well on their way to prosperity.

Dior's iconic new ready-to-wear design had arrived in Paris in the late 1940s and now that the war was over, the style was on every woman's mind, and nearly every woman owned a tight sweater and bullet bra to give her that conical-shaped bust.

Mrs Campbell was determined to make a Lady out of Amalie. She was expected to master complex feasts, set an impeccable dinner table, and host a dinner party without defiance including being the object of admiration among the male guests.

Evenings at the manor would include nights of poetry recitals, enchanting performances of piano, and dance. Amalie's feeble excuses fell on deaf ears.

'You have to change,' Mrs Campbell would say. 'A magical evening is bestowed before us.'

Amalie's performance was delivered with clarity and passion. The audience cheered, and for the first time, Amalie smiled. The performance was over, and she basked in her success. The guests bid farewell.

Amalie began to show a willingness to leave her anger behind. She was to be judged ferociously on her social protocol and was to be assessed by a formidable guest. She was to display poise and composure without seemingly to try too hard. That would be fatal. She entertained with gracefulness and ease, and most of the time she accomplished all of this with a smile both on her lips and in her eyes.

For Mrs Campbell, the devil was in the detail.

CHAPTER 11

"We all go a little mad sometimes."
Norman Bates

The 1950s saw Britain through huge social and economic changes. The emergence of rock 'n' roll music and coffee houses suited the ever-exciting East End.

Britain was working hard to boost the new decade. *"We've done wonders since the war, and now we're blowing our own trumpet for a change,"* the radio sounded.

A cascade of gadgets found themselves into homes, and Amalie was fascinated by collapsible cake tins, meat thermometers, and supersized grills. Amalie had a new dressing table with three compartments, and Uncle William purchased a new television so he could watch *Panorama* during the cold rainy evenings.

It would take a few more years before Britain would have successful colour television due to post-war austerity, much to William's dismay, and his American comrades were more than happy to flaunt that the United States had become the world's strongest military power, their economy was booming and the fruits of this prosperity resulted in new cars, suburban houses, and a variety of consumer goods that were available to more people than ever before. Even though in Britain business soared, for many the 1950s were a constant struggle to feed large families with the meagre rations that were still in force. Parents had to juggle working lives with bringing up children and still had to queue for the basic necessities.

Through the bustling streets of the East End, William took Amalie to a place like none other before. She left the pretty flower beds, the manicured lawns, and the wrought iron gate to grungy crowded streets of London. Amalie followed her uncle through the East End streets towards their destination – a surprise for Amalie.

'Whoa, that's a pretty ocean pearl right there.'

'Oh er, wouldn't mind dipping ma wick in that there.'

The market-goers sniggered and laughed as Amalie and her uncle passed by. One chewed on a toothpick as he glared at Amalie head to toe.

'What are they saying, Uncle?'

'Never you mind yourself with such filth,' he answered.

One of the men heard and lifted his head, 'Oi you ain't a kerb crawler are ya?'

William turned around and stood in front of Amalie ensuring she was out of sight. 'We don't want trouble.'

'Ay, Don, we got a Barney Rubble here.'

'Honestly, not the case.' William tried to diffuse the situation.

'Let's have a look at her thruppenny bits then, kerb crawler.'

Amalie had never heard her uncle swear before and today was no different as he answered, 'Why don't you do a Vincent Van Gogh.'

'Got ourselves a Mockney, Don – get em.'

Amalie and her uncle ran, her lungs began to burn as she ran as hard as she could, ensuring her uncle was close. The footsteps of their pursuers echoed so much neither Amalie nor her uncle could tell whether they were near or just behind them. She snatched a look behind her, the fleeting blurred glimpse and sudden terror came to a sudden halt as they ran into a building, and they cowered in the darkness. Both their hearts hammered through their chests whilst listening for the fine leather click of the Italian shoes that pursued them, but nothing. They smiled and laughed while catching their breath.

'Who were they?' she asked.

'They, Amalie, were cockneys; being born within earshot of the bells of St Mary-Le-Bow, Cheapside, in the City of London (known as the Bow bells).

'I didn't understand a word they said.'

'That's the idea! The language was invented in London in the 1840s by market traders, costermongers (sellers of fruit and vegetables from handcarts) and street hawkers.'

'Why?'

'Hearsay has it that the criminal underworld in London developed their own secret language to confuse and become incomprehensible to authorities and anyone else eavesdropping in on their business.'

'Interesting...'

Amalie and her uncle continued to head towards their destination whilst looking over their shoulders.

'We had better get a cab if we are going to make it on time; I *had* hoped to have shown you around.'

The Bow-street entrance was satisfyingly old and

very rococo in its original decor, as much as the Covent Garden entrance embraced the 20th century wholeheartedly. The Royal Opera House could be described by some as unsavoury, and Uncle William informed Amalie that even one London journalist described it as "a sordid building, hideous, smoke begrimed and uncouth, set among sordid slums". At the time, fifty years ago, he may have been right: the area was full of slums, horse manure, and rotting vegetables.

After finding their seats, Amalie and William were accompanied by other high profile guests – acquaintances of William.

'Oh, you will thoroughly enjoy the play, Amalie. It's about a man with radical contradictions. He's tender yet ferocious and reckless yet cautious.'

As the lights dimmed and the show started, it became evident to Amalie that the main great themes of life; war, love and death are also the three themes in literature. Amalie became fascinated at Shakespeare's exploration of death in almost every play she studied thereafter. His plays exhibited every conceivable way of dying, as if it is an integral part and idea of the play. Like Amalie, plagues and death that decimated the country in Shakespeare's time shaped a culture in which death played a recurring role in daily life. Images of death and deceit, bountiful in the form of art in an era of high mortality rates and mass death due to war and where whole villages were wiped out for no reason, were seen as an act of God: a punishment to the people. Amalie looked around the theatre, she studied society's attempt to comprehend the real danger being portrayed on stage that pandered to the audience's taste for death and violence in despicable ways.

Amalie in the past had contemplated suicide but restrained herself from fear of eternal suffering - should there be an afterlife. Her fascination with death developed into an obsession, and she realised that even the most vibrant of human beings, in the end, are reduced to dust. Death becomes the generator of nature in which human beings are thus recycled and provide the lands with fertiliser and nutrition. She neither feared nor longed for death, but she accepted that without it, there cannot be life.

As the play came to an end, it left Amalie with more questions than answers about deception and moral ambiguity. Like Amalie, Hamlet had depicted a character haunted by the past but immobilised by the future. Amalie was a stranger to the world, and she was deeply unsure of what it hid. Her nightmares convinced Amalie that a ghost that bore the face of her brother was there to help plot revenge. Her mourning turned to rage, and she began to plot her revenge on those that did her and her family wrong. She was thrown into multiple dilemmas of who she could trust. She negotiated friends, family, and many that possessed ulterior motives. What role would she play in the course of justice? Amalie became consumed with the awful machinations of thinking itself. She was torn between thought and action. Was her madness part of her performance, or was she on the brink of insanity?

The crowd cheered, it was unnaturally loud but the claps, whistles, and joyous crowd rubbed shoulders with one another. The atmosphere was joyful, people were happy; it created a sense of elation, a performance well done. The actors bowed and the cacophony of applause created an infectious outpour of emotion. People cried, they stomped their feet, they whistled and shook each other's hands. There was something magical about the performance of the play and being among the crowd; everyone in unison acted the same, they felt emotions at the same time, their faces expressed the same thoughts and Amalie smiled for a brief moment at that feeling of acceptance.

The lady beside William leaned towards her and shouted over the intense volume.

'Did you enjoy that, Dear?'

'I did very much,' Amalie answered.

'Sorry what did you say?' the lady beckoned.

'Yes, are you deaf?' Amalie smiled. The lady's face portrayed her confusion, and William interrupted.

'She said, "More so than Macbeth".'

'Amalie dear, you look flushed? Are you well?' The woman asked.

'Yes, it's just this theatre, I love it. Will you excuse me?' Amalie asked as she stood and curtsied.

'Certainly,' the lady answered. 'Does she suffer from fever, Lord William?'

'She suffers from too much rouge.' The woman's husband interrupted.

'Nonsense, a Lady does not wear blush.' Lord William stated.

'No, a Lady does not.'

IV

STAFFORDSHIRE, ENGLAND

CHAPTER 12

*"It's the hardest thing of all, to let someone go
that you love."*

Night in the heart of Stafford was inky darkness that
sank to the marrow of Inspector John Owen's bones.
The attacks of lightning steadily made their way
throughout the city. A jagged streak of energy
descended near the surrounding buildings and
temporarily held the residents prisoners in their own
homes. Inspector Owen sat in his black and white
Hillman Minx and counted the explosions in the night
sky. The noise level became loud and intense, rattling
the car windows, and his heart pounded inside his
chest. Inspector Owen started the car and drove
towards Stoke Minster; a spectacular historic building
set among several acres of greenery and the new
location for the resident trouble makers. But, tonight
is too tumultuous for troublesome love-sick
adolescents. As the rain held off, Inspector Owen
stood beside his car and emerged from the shadows
inflicted by the street lights. His black raincoat
dripped from the rain before the lightning struck, and
his pale face turned towards the minster's light.

'I hope you'd be proud of me, father,' he
whispered as he stood on the very spot where his
father had been found shot in the head. It was blunt
and brutal. Owen remembered the incident like it was
yesterday.

His father was on his way home after shift with

little John on the back seat. He pulled the car over, and John watched his father exit the car and walk towards the Minster. He turned to look back at the car and raised a hand to indicate that John should stay put. As he disappeared into the shadows, the echo of an ear-splitting BANG rippled and sliced through the air. That was the last time John saw his father alive.

John remembered his father's glasses always sat too low on the bridge of his nose and often obscured eye contact when people spoke to him. That wasn't often as they found him eccentric and intimidating, but he had one hell of a talent at catching perps; for this reason, John wanted to be just like his father – a police officer.

Inspector Owen returned frequently to this place hoping for direction, a sign from his father where his life should lead. He thought about the next day when he would become DCI Owen.

The promotion was made possible through his help in the hunt for serial killer John Christie. Every available police officer was on call for a countrywide manhunt for Christie after bodies were discovered at his flat by his landlord.

John Christie was a British sequence killer and necrophile that murdered at least eight people during the 1940s and 1950s – including his wife – by strangling them at his flat in London. His first victim that he admitted to had been Ruth Fuerst; a 21-year-old Austrian munitions worker and part-time prostitute. That money supplemented her income. After inviting her to his home and engaging sexually, Christie impulsively strangled her on his bed, stowed her body beneath the floorboards in his living room, and buried the body in the garden the following evening.

Christie was a police officer during WW2 despite having served time in prison for theft and assault, and had befriended Timothy Evans and his wife. Years later when the capture of Timothy Evans resulted in his offering a forced false confession to placing his wife's remains in the drain, it sent three police officers to conduct a search. But, lack of expertise in handling forensic evidence caused several mistakes in handling the case, especially in overlooking remains such as a femur propping up a fence, and allowed Christie to continue his reign of terror.

It took the jury three days to find Evans guilty, and Christie wasn't even considered a suspect. The fact he had been in the police force served him well and was something the jury found respectable. The garden to Christie's residence had been very small, roughly 5x4.5 meters, and had the search been conducted effectively, the investigation would have exposed Christie as the murderer, not Evans and the lives of Christie's future four victims may have been spared.

Tourists were rife during the '40s and '50s – wanting to see the changing of the guards, which happened daily at Buckingham Palace when the king was at home, even a dog cemetery, and sheep kept in Green park as a reminder of the countryside in a modern city were reasons to visit London, and tourists would remember posters plastered among other posters advertising camping holidays. During the '50s people had little chance to go on exotic holidays, and caravanning became the easiest way to escape day to day tribulations. Even a few days were an opportunity to have fun.

"A few days by the sea is a thing tackled by different people in different ways: to some, it is a panic-stricken rush to the railway station with bulging suitcases and to others, it is a car crammed with buckets, spades and fretful children. But to many modern young couples the trip seems to be simplicity itself. In a matter of minutes, the trailer and dingy are in position and the family transport is all ready to go. And if you're wondering why a dingy needs a streamline trailer we should explain that it's really a collapsible caravan. The caravan built at Emsworth, Hampshire is not complicated and even a moron, mechanically speaking can fix it up in a matter of minutes and it provides comfortable accommodation for two adults and a child".

Among these advertisements were posters warning tourists of Christie's whereabouts, and Inspector Owen worked like a man crazed. He called a contact at Scotland Yard who had been involved on his father's case to learn everything there was to know about profiling murderers and methods used by profilers. Due to the lack of female officers in the force, Owen accompanied many male associates in stakeouts posing as loved up couples in an attempt to catch the perp at large. Christie was apprehended ten days after the hunt began.

John Owen had many liaisons with members of the opposite sex during his adulthood, but none, in particular, stood the test of time or were particularly special. He rarely would make any long-lasting relationships with either men or women, and he maintained no friendship with anyone since the death of his father. However, he had a strong relationship with his mother, and she maintained that through all her faults in life, John was the one thing she got right.

When he was not working, he entertained himself with swimming and his excellence in running proved a useful skill on the job. He would never consider himself a race car driver – although one of the main reasons he became a police officer on traffic was to drive the latest Jaguar S Type; its independent rear suspension helped it manoeuvre around corners with ease, even on uneven surfaces. And, although it proved a popular getaway vehicle for criminals, Owen's natural driving talent gave him an edge.

MI6 had been particularly interested in Owen's ability to gain information. He appeared to possess a unique ability to analyse his environment and people, and therefore was prepared for any hostile reaction that may occur. He was to be a valued asset as many other agents lacked language skills; Owen's interest in the performing arts had led him to learn languages including French and Spanish, although his Russian was passable.

Owen was at the peak of his life, and his body was regimented like that of a Marine. For Owen, it wasn't difficult to use psychological tricks on women to gain information when he had a body to go alongside it. But, since the death of his father, Owen felt that he never wanted to feel vulnerable and showed remarkable skill at stealth: moving quickly and quietly through the enemy ground during training. MI6 concluded that, should it be necessary, Owen would easily be capable of killing a man in a crowded place without ever being noticed.

Steve Harrison read through Owen's report. John hadn't received any military training, but he excelled in all areas of weapon handling. He had excellent precision, reaction, and speed. Although not yet tried, Harrison imagined he would easily become accustomed to handling machine guns, though not required, not soon anyway. It was noted in the report that three years ago, Owen's firearms trainer had stated, "Owen's accuracy is unmatched and his ability to switch between weapons with great speed, to shoot moving targets whilst in varying positions was second to none." The trainer's final statement finished with, "to save lives, we police officers must be taught to think beyond the gun belt".

The Chief of Stafford Police, who had recommended John Owen to MI6, had not even considered anyone else for the position. Owen was a quiet and modest unique individual with a sound mind and spirit. Most of the other officers were completely unaware of his intelligence and thought of him as arrogant and conceited but like many that lose a family member when they're young, Owen had abandonment issues. He professed once to the Chief of Police on a drunken evening that he had never fallen in love. It was the first time the C.O.P had seen Owen reveal anything personal about himself, and it was never brought up in conversation again.

Owen was a man of habit and thrived under pressure and new challenges. But, he would often rebel against the structure. He is despised by colleagues for his unorthodox methods of closing a case, and while Harrison finished up reading the report, he thought to himself: Owen was perfect.

CHAPTER 13

"The dead won't bother you; it's the living you
have to worry about."
John Wayne Gacy

Christie had been a sublime suspect. He confessed that "all my life I've had this fear of appearing ridiculous as a lover", and psychologists theorised that Christie had formed this hatred for women after being ridiculed during his adolescence about his sexual inadequacies.

Having an IQ of 128 put Christie into the smartest 5% of the nation, and he had high hope of achievement. But, during his marriage, he was convicted of several crimes including theft from a post office, violence, larceny, and the assault of a prostitute. After being released from prison he reconciled with his wife but after suffering a miscarriage their relationship began to deteriorate. His urges to relieve his increasingly violent sexual tendencies continued, and he mistakenly had an affair with a female officer at the police station where he worked, resulting in a sound beating by her husband when he found out. Christie's wife backed up his lies, leading to the police pointing the finger at an innocent man; Evans.

Inspector Owen had been chasing Kathleen Maloney all over the country after she committed crime after crime. During 1950 she was jailed for one month for being drunk and disorderly, and the following year she was again charged for a similar offence. Described as 5ft 2", dyed blonde hair with a plump face and hazel eyes, she also had five children, and whilst one had been adopted, the others were in a children's home. After her family turned their back on Kathleen, she hitchhiked to London as she was "fed up because the police were always chasing her". One friend noted that Kathleen had no home and went with any man she could find, and she was often seen loitering outside pubs smiling at American soldiers. She was later picked up when found sleeping in public toilets. It was around this time she encountered a man, aged around 50 of medium height with a big nose that "sort of licked his lips when he spoke to Kathleen". Maureen Briggs revealed that she met up with Christie when he offered money to photograph her in "various positions in the nude", and after taking a great many photographs, he proceeded to give them a pound each for their efforts.

Christie confessed that when the pair approached him for more money, he claimed: "I walked away, but she followed and pushed into my house. I asked her to leave but she went into the kitchen and began to undress. I thought, *alright...If ever a woman deserved to die, you do"*.

Inspector Owen had not ever dreamed that poor Kathleen would become victim to one of the country's most notorious killing sprees. Christie later claimed, "it was little Kathy I felt sorry for. She was a sweet kid. I felt sorry for her".

Christie was found under Putney Bridge in London by Inspectors Owen and Reese; Owen remembered the moment clear as day.

"We've been sat here for hours," PC Reese *moaned. Inspector Owen sighed and looked out the window for signs of Christie after an anonymous tip placed him at the location.*

"Are you going to whine all evening, PC Reese?"

"Wind your fuckin' neck in will ya, Owen!"

"I'm going to ignore that remark – being your superior..."

"You know what your problem is, Owen..."

"That's Inspector Owen to you."

"Your problem is you need to get out more."

"I'm doing just fine the way I am...thank you for your concern. If we can turn our attention back to the matter at hand?"

"10-4!"

"10-4?" Owen raises a brow... "At ease Reese, it's just us here."

"I think I see something."

Inspector Owen picked up the radio and rang through for back up. He could see a man fitting Christie's description. "I'm going in."

"Shouldn't we wait?"

"We don't have time, wait here."

"No one wants a fuckin' hero, Owen, Inspector..." Owen exited the vehicle, leaving Reese inside.

As Owen approached the suspect he asked, "Excuse me, Sir, can you take off your hat? I think you need to come with me, Mr Christie."

The Daily Mirror's headlines stated:

CHRISTIE IS CHARGED WITH MURDER

John Reginald Halliday Christie, 55, of Rillington Place, Notting Hill, West London was charged last night with the murder of his wife, Mrs Ethel Christie, 54, whose body was found buried under the floorboards at no.10 Rillington-Place, last Wednesday.

Christie will appear at West London magistrates' court today.

DCI Owen often found it easier to keep a freshly laundered suit at the office, in case he worked a late shift. All his suits followed the same cut and shape but varied in colour from greys to blacks and navy blue and he'd get them laundered two or three at a time so he had a fresh suit available, just in case. And he'd keep three white shirts on hangers there, too, regularly changing throughout the day.

Owen preferred to work on his own because he didn't need to confer anything with anyone, and if PC Reese knew about Owen's extracurricular activities, it was almost certain he would squeal to the superintendent and put an end to it.

But it was near the holiday period and PC Reese had taken an early holiday; Owen was free to make his own moves.

Owen stood in front of the mirror in the bathroom at headquarters of the Staffordshire Police Station fastening the last button of his clean suit. He ran his hand over his unruly hair combing it into place behind his ears. It was all he could do but it went well with his five o'clock shadow and made him look more like a hard nut than a ponce.

It was June, 1953, and upon leaving the station, Owen picked up a copy of the Daily Mirror with the image of a sorrowful mother of Tim Evans. The front page stated:

CHRISTIE
HE WAITS TO DIE WHERE EVANS DIED

Of course, that's all that was needed to inform Owen that Christie had been sentenced to death by hanging.

Christie was hanged on 15th July, 1953, at Pentonville Prison by executioner Albert Pierrepoint, who had ironically also hanged innocent Evans. After being pinioned for his execution, it was said that Christie complained that his nose itched at which Pierrepoint assured him that, "it won't bother you for long". Albert Pierrepoint undertook his first lead execution in 1941, and came from a long line of official hangmen. His role included the clause:

He should clearly understand that his conduct and general behaviour should be respectable, not only at the place and time of the execution, but before and subsequently, that he should avoid attracting public attention in going to or from the prison, and he is prohibited from giving to any personal particulars on the subject of his duty for publication.

Owen recalled the day of Christie's death and not for a split second doubted himself regardless of PC Plonker's plea to remain in the car. Based on the pubic hair collected by Christie, it was speculated that he was responsible for far more murders than those he carried out at 10 Rillington Place. Christie claimed that the four different clumps of pubic hair were from his wife and the three bodies police discovered, but only one sample matched on the bodies, and that was

Ethel Christie.

During Christie's final interview, Inspector Owen asked him, *"Did you kill Mrs Evans? What about the baby?"*

"Let me assure you, Inspector, I've been quite ill, I honestly cannot remember."

"They say you killed the baby. The jury will have you hung, drawn and quartered."

"I have tended to black out now and then. You can't hang a man surely who's not in charge of his faculties?"

"Say their names."

"I'm sorry to interrupt, Inspector, but we're ready." John Owen left the room and he never saw Christie again.

Even if the clumps of hair matched the bodies of Fuerst and Eady (which had by then decomposed into skeletons) there was still a hair sample unaccounted for as Beryl Evans still had all her hair intact.

It was something Owen wanted to pursue; to trace the other victims of Christie, but no attempts were made to further the investigation. As far as the police were concerned, they had their man and case closed. It was out of Owen's hands.

In 1941, Pierrepoint hanged gangland killer and nightclub owner Antonio "Babe" Mancini. He'd be told the height and weight of his prisoner, view the condemned man through a Judas-hole in the door to judge the man's build, and then proceed to the execution room which was usually next to the condemned man's cell. Pierrepoint would test the equipment using a sack containing roughly the same weight as the prisoner, calculate the length of rope he'd need, and lift the weighted sack by pulling on the rope. He'd ensure the rope was stretched, and it would then be readjusted the following morning if necessary.

The next morning Pierrepoint would enter the cell at 08.00 am, and with a leather strap, he would secure the condemned man's arms behind his back. They, plus Pierrepoint's assistant and two prison officers would walk to the execution chamber. Pierrepoint would place a white hood over the prisoner's head and a noose around his neck and the metal eye through which the rope was looped; Pierrepoint would then place the knot under the man's left jawbone. When the prisoner dropped through the trap door, the metal eye would ensure the head snapped back and the neck was broken in one swift manoeuvre. There was a right way and a wrong way to hang a man, and Pierrepoint's method from strapping the man's arms and opening the trap door took him roughly twelve seconds. Mancini reportedly shouted "Cheerio" as he dropped.

Pierrepoint was a respected hangman and during his tenure, he hanged over two hundred war criminals as well as other high profile murderers including John Haigh - the Acid Bath Murderer. Owen remembered that day, too, and how the massive trap doors on the gallows in London's Wandsworth Prison flung open, sending the noosed vampire murderer to his doom. Pierrepoint and his assistant had no knowledge that at that moment they had just executed one of the most chilling and ingenious murderers of the times. The tabloids had been filled with sensational headlines about the Acid Bath Murderer who had claimed the lives of nine people and disposed of their bodies in an oil drum of sulphuric acid. He claimed to drink the blood of his victims, too, before reducing their bodies to sludge. It wasn't surprising that the press was all over Haigh with his confession of acid baths and drinking blood, so the Daily Mirror announced the crimes on its front page on Thursday, the 3rd of March, 1949.

"Vampire horror in London, SW7"

Steve Harrison had been one of the crime squad working late on the vampire case, and he often would mention the newspaper clipping now hanging in his office that stated: "For the first time in the Yard's century-old history, detectives were following clues leading to a maniac who – like the vampire of Eastern European folk-lore – drank his victim's blood". Harrison would joke and say "one minute I was booking a bunch of bastard sex traffickers then I'm yanked off that and put onto this. Every available man was working late that night".

Owen recalled the news article, but it was something different to hear a first account of the scene from someone who had been there at the time. Harrison had mentioned on the quiet to Owen, "It was like nothing else, I remember it as clear as day, a cold chilly February of 1949. We raided this warehouse on Leopold Road in West Sussex that was owned by the defendant and we found forty-gallon drums of concentrated sulphuric acid. I mean who has that? But no, it gets worse, this fuck had twenty-eight pounds of melted human fat, of course, we didn't know that at the time but by shitin' heck it stank! Oh and yeah the human foot and dentures we found was kind of a giveaway what shit show we had stumbled on - Haigh murdered someone and dissolved their body in acid to try and hide his crime. Who'd of thought this man, with the world his oyster? He grew up in an affluent family in Yorkshire and attended classical music concerts, he was even awarded scholarships. You just don't know who your neighbours are these days".

"But where on earth would someone get the idea to dissolve someone in an acid bath?" Owen implored at the time, at which Harrison answered, "Well, whilst he was serving time in prison for a theft he began reading books from the prison library. He became obsessed with Georges-Alexandre Sarret who was a French murderer who had dissolved his victims in sulphuric acid. Don't ask me how but he managed to get some samples of sulphuric acid whilst in prison and then pay other inmates to bring him dead mice to conduct his experiments on," Harrison shrugged.

Owen shook his head, "Just imagine how many people would not have died if he hadn't read about it. That literally inspired a copycat murderer."

"It's just the way the cookie crumbles, Owen."

"It's a morbidly attractive idea that establishes a path of action for someone with murderous tendencies. Don't you think that creating this vicious cycle of covering such killings just fuels the interest of would-be murderers?"

"What are you getting at, Owen?"

"I'm just saying we should pay special attention to how the press portrays these murderers. I mean, some people are funny creatures; the last thing we would want is them portrayed like some kind of celebrity hero."

The following months were magical and widely celebrated. The newspaper couldn't get enough of Inspector Owen, and the press hung on his every word. He was invited to afternoon tea surrounded by the upper crust – surrounded by well to do's and their eclectic treasures inside their country homes.

Owen discovered a hidden world of decadence and luxury, and he quickly became fascinated at these medieval fortified castles that now evolved for comfort rather than defence. These houses were built to impress and entertain important guests, and Owen was mesmerised as he witnessed aristocrats striving to out-do one another in the opulence of their homes. There were a variety of designs, extravagantly decorated with French and Italian furnishings.

Stately homes were power symbols owned by the country's leading noblemen. Inspector Owen had dreamed of homes like these where a rigid hierarchy conducted a plethora of team members that were responsible for the day to day upkeep. He came across butlers, housekeepers, private tutors, and a head chef that would prepare some of the most elaborate meals he had ever come across, and one meal stuck firmly in his mind – not necessarily the food itself but by whom it was served.

CHAPTER 14

*"To live is the rarest thing in the world. Most
people exist, that is all." Oscar Wilde.*

It was the 6th of February, 1952, and the news
announced the death of King George VI. Britain
mourns. The people mourned over a Monarch whose
life was an inspiration to all over whom he ruled, and
William listened hard into the radio as the words were
spoken, "It is with the greatest sorrow that we make
the following announcement. It was announced from
Sandringham at 10.45 today the 6th of February,
1952, that the King who retired to rest last night in his
usual health passed peacefully away in his sleep,
earlier this morning".

The flags were lowered in tribute. High over Big
Ben the flag was low as the news spread that the King
was dead. The news spread like wildfire to the
furthest corners of Britain, and the heart of the
nation's people stopped. *This cannot be.*

William and Amalie attended Westminster Abbey
with their anonymous prayers among others. Crowds
gathered in front of Buckingham Palace like they had
done just four months before when news circulated
that the King was seriously ill; Operation on the King,
the newspapers had read. The King was gravely ill
and the nation prayed, but now, the King was dead.

Amalie, too, mourned, for it was the King of
England that supported Winston Churchill throughout
the war and even visited armies on battlefronts. He

was a symbolic leader to the British people and he boosted morale by visiting munitions factories and bomb sites and had famously quoted, "Like so many of our people, we have now had a personal experience of German barbarity which only strengthens the resolution of all of us to fight through to final victory."

The country was in a state of shock as they reminisced about that September day in 1939 the British Empire and commonwealth declared war on Nazi Germany. The King and Queen stayed in London during the mass air attacks and German bombing in 1940 and 1941, even though on the first night of the Blitz it killed one thousand civilians, mostly in the East End. King George VI was seen as sharing the hardship among the common people and therefore his popularity soared, and Britain and its allies became victorious in 1945. Even though during the war, Prime Minister Winston Churchill showed courage, perseverance, independence, and emotional resilience, on the death of King George, his friend, his words were moving in their sincerity and sorrow.

"During these last months, the King walked with death as if death were a companion, an acquaintance whom he recognised and did not fear. In the end, death came as a friend and after a happy day of sunshine and sport, and after "good night" to those who loved him best, he fell asleep as every man or woman who strives to fear God and nothing else in the world may hope to do". William listened intently to Churchill's speech. Churchill had rallied the people and led the country from the brink of defeat in the Second World War to victory, and shaped the allied strategy in the war. In the early stages of the Second World War, Churchill had very few weapons. He attacked the opposition with words, powerful speeches, some of the most defiant and heroic words with hints of humour ever heard in the English language and they reached out to everyone in Britain and across Nazi-occupied Europe offering hope – he figuratively sent speeches into battle. His speech on the death of King George VI did not fail and people listened, for he had "nothing to offer but blood, toil, tears and sweat". Churchill was William's inspiration and icon of admiration.

The young new Queen's coronation took place sixteen months after the mourning of her father, King George VI. Out of respect, holding a festival such as a coronation would be disrespectful to have been held during the country's mourning.

The televised event of the coronation of Queen Elizabeth was watched by almost 20 million people crowded around less than 3 million TV sets. From that day, television became the heart of families spread across Britain. Looking stylish after years of clothes rationing was important again, and French designer Dior brought his latest creations to London in 1953 – putting an accent on colours, and Uncle William was one of the first to order a *Vie de Chateau*, a dinner ensemble in embroidered black velvet, for his favourite niece.

Four days after her coronation, the Queen made her first public appearance at Epsom Racecourse, and Amalie and her uncle watched as her horse took second place. In the 50s, Britain had come close to the country's dream of full employment; however, the country's affluence began to take a downward spiral when the manufacturing industry was developing fast and the automotive industry was increasing productivity by leaps and bounds. The need to be competitive, combined with the new technology, meant that the industry simply did not need as many workers. It had been encouraged to reduce the price of motorcars when the country was facing strong competition from the world market. As time progressed, machines needed fewer and fewer men to work them, and a crisis was now upon Britain causing strikes in protest.

But, television on the rainy evenings announced a new explosion that offered the people a distraction. A young handsome man by the name of Elvis Presley exploded onto the British music scene, and huge crowds gathered to see him at the station.

'May I change channel, Uncle?'

'Of course.'

'Fanny Craddock!'

'Are you going to be creating swans with Mrs Campbell for our next event, Amalie?'

'Do you think our guests would appreciate my little ingenuity of turning piped cream into swans on their hard-boiled eggs?'

'Feathers might fly if not!'

The butler knocked gently on the door, 'Excuse me, Sir, but there is a gentleman named John outside. Shall I tell him to come back at another time?'

'Of course not! Send him through.' William stood. 'Amalie, dear, can you please excuse me for a moment.'

Amalie stood from her position on the chaise,

nodded and walked to exit the room and bumped into Owen. 'Oh my gosh, I'm so sorry,' and she shuffled away.

DCI Owen smiled as his eyes followed Amalie into the other room. *'Who is that wonderful creature?'* he asked himself as Amalie disappeared from view.

'Owen, dear chap! Or is it Detective Chief Inspector now? Congratulations. I almost didn't recognise you without your uniform.'

'Thank you. How are the books coming along?

I picked up the latest newspaper on the way here.' Owen fingered the front page.

'Splendid. That's another murdering scallywag on the front page to add to the ever-growing pile of newspapers; who is the bastard this time?'

'Christie.'

'Oh...*that* scoundrel.'

'What's the latest on your recent publication?'

'It's a New York Times best-seller thanks to your input.'

'Congratulations.'

'Congratulations are for us both. This deserves a drink! Mrs Campbell,' William bellowed, 'bring the *Veuve Clicquot*.'

William and Owen had become good friends since he attended an event held at Lord William's. His invaluable knowledge in return helped William accurately write detective stories with authenticity and quid pro quo, William's friends in high places made sure to look after Owen but by no means aided in his promotion.

'At least you won't have to work alongside PC

Plonker any longer? He seems like a brick short? And rude.'

'Indeed.'

DCI Owen scanned the room taking in the Italian accents of William's furnishings and carefully selected a book from the coffee table *The Divine Comedy*.'

'Oh, that's Amalie's. Please be careful – she's awfully peculiar with people meddling with her belongings.'

'Amalie? What a beautiful name.'

'Yes, my niece.'

'Was that the young lady that I saw?'

'Yes, I'd certainly hope so. It's not too often young women grace my presence.'

William stood very still as Amalie appeared. '"He listens well who takes notes".'

'Amalie, this is my friend John.'

'"So gentle seems my lady and so pure when she greets anyone, that scarce the eye: Such modesty and brightness can endure, and the tongue, trembling, falters in reply".'

'John....I'm lost for words. I didn't know you read!' William shockingly stated.

'I've dabbled. My mother often lectured at the Library. Anyway, it has been a pleasure. Amalie, it has been an honour.' *"For she doth make my veins and pulses tremble".*

Everyone that attended Detective Owen's funeral held their heads low. Maybe they were showing their respect? Maybe they didn't want to acknowledge their fate. After all, there are only two certainties in life and those were death and taxes.

The coffin was pulled out from a wooden carved panel hearse by four men all wearing suits. Silence pervaded as John's father was carried to his place of rest. John held his mother's hand the whole time and helped wipe away her tears as she wept. John, as young as he was, replayed that night over and over wondering if he could have done anything different that would have changed his father's outcome. He looked towards the sky; its colour was like a spring day, offensively bright and cheerful. He frowned thinking the world had conspired to continue without his father, and John felt angered that it wasn't dull and drizzly like his emotions.

"Come on dear, we must say our goodbyes. Your father wouldn't want us to cry anymore," John's mother said as she struggled to hold back her tears as she unwillingly acknowledged the finality of her husband's death. The coffin lowered into the freshly dug soil in the ground, and a new onslaught of tears followed steadily and silently down each person's face. "Goodbye, Dad," little John waved whilst gripping tightly his mother's hand.

Owen's mother never did get over her husband's death. John would hear her crying with grief as it surged with every expelled breath, but with a young child to raise she threw herself straight into employment at the local library, often bringing home several books at a time to read to John before bed. She explained to him later in life that reading was an escape from reality. She'd get so drawn into an enthralling story that she would forget her surroundings, her imagination took over, and she could create this entire literary world where her characters would look and behave just as she wanted. John was absorbed from that moment on.

V

STOCKSEE,
WEST GERMANY

CHAPTER 15

*Revenge sounds so severe, that's why I prefer to
call it "Returning the favour".*

The premature release of Helga Oppenheimer made
TV and newspaper headlines. She was released only
ten years into her twenty-year sentence due to good
behaviour.

Uncle William shared stories with DCI Owen and
word had it she was now in Stocksee, near Kiel in
West Germany practising as a family doctor.

'Promise me, Amalie, you will leave this alone.'
William begged Amalie.

'I can't make those kinds of promises.'

'You've just started a new life for yourself. Please
darling, you've got everything going for you.'

'If you love me you will let me go.'

'OK, but I'm paying for your flight.'

'Flight?' she questioned.

'Yes, no arguing. It's perfectly safe.'

These years were known as the Golden Age of
Flying and were the era of sumptuous design. The
flying experience was like nothing else – from the
visual appearance of the cabin to the silverware and
the stewardess's uniforms that had to have been the
imagination of some high profile designer. Amalie
didn't want to even imagine what her uncle had paid
for this opportunity; to her, this exorbitant amount of
money was wasted. She didn't mind at all hitching a
ride here and there to reach her destination, but her

uncle wouldn't have it any other way. The pneumatic germ tube stunk of vomit and smoke, and the only potential relief from the travelling was the very possible prospect of her own death.

A family of three were in the next row across, and although Amalie looked like the perfect passenger, her blood vessels began to bulge, her face reddened ever so slightly and the proverbial steam was about to come out of her ears. She held herself in complete tension.

'Excuse me, can you please quieten down?' she asked.

'We're going on holiday,' the father sniggered.

'I couldn't give a rat's.'

'Get bent will ya?'

Amalie groaned and raised an eyebrow.

'Good   evening,   this   is your   Captain speaking. Thank you for flying with us. There has been a small problem in the lavatory so I inform you that we are now turning on the "Fasten Seat Belt" sign, and we ask you to please remain seated or return to your seats as we prepare for landing. Thank you.'

Fifteen minutes before landing the cabin erupted. A body had been found in the lavatory. Apparently the deceased had been experiencing a series of bloody coughs, defecation and vomiting. He was pronounced dead at 30,000 ft. Amalie finally had a few minutes to herself.

When she landed, Amalie broke out in a cold sweat, feet firmly on the ground. Northern Germany was a world apart from England although it shared its green fields and farmland. She hitched a ride into Braunschweig, and a cold shiver descended her back as she read: WILLKOMMEN.

'Halte hier. Vielen Dank.' *Stop here, thank you.* Amalie instructed the driver.

'Bist du sicher? Ich kann dich weiter in die Stadt bringen.' *Are you sure? I can take you further into the town.*

'Ich muss nicht weiter gehen.' *I don't need to go any further.*

Amalie swallowed hard as she exited the driver's car just two hours away from her destination – Braunschweig. The town lies on the Oker River and legend has it that it was founded by Bruno, son of Duke Ludolf of Saxony. The town had suffered severely before being captured by allied forces in 1945, and slowly the people were rebuilding it. Medieval buildings that survived included the 12th-century Romanesque cathedral of St. Blasius which contained the tombs of its founder, and on the castle square is the bronze lion monument – the emblem of Braunschweig carved in 1166 as a symbol of Henry the Lion.

Braunschweig was also famous for its sausages, asparagus and gingerbread, and many locals recommended a nearby tavern for a bite to eat.

'Good afternoon, I'd like something to warm me up?' Amalie asked.

The men inside roared with laughter and several stood up to walk towards Amalie. Her head turned a one-eighty, and she pierced them with a look.

'If you can drink this pretty lady, it's free,' the bartender offered, slamming a schnapps on the bar top. He had a barrel chest that curved outwards and he smiled.

'What is it?' she queried.

'Ratzeputz,' he answered.

Amalie heard rumours that this was the hardest liquor around, "*Mind cleaner*", and if you could stomach this then you were more than likely to earn respect from the locals. If the mere alcohol content was the only thing that enchanted you and drew you to indulge in such a drink, then you could source alternative types of concentrated ethanol at risk of burning your innards. But, nothing yet could beat this north German firewater.

Amalie observed the small glass in front of her. Sure, it looked innocuous enough – a light brown colour resembling brandy or cognac, no different than what uncle William would sip on. The bartender's eyes had a nasty gleam as he stared with hunger. Amalie took the glass and swallowed a hefty swig. It hit her throat like dynamite, and a fireball ignited as it sent a blazing river to her stomach. Amalie kept eye contact slamming the glass down in front of her.

'Another,' she demanded, 'in fact, I'll take the bottle.' Should Amalie need to reduce and not murder her large circle of so-called friends back in Surrey, then this ginger liquor would be a great additive to the family's punch recipe.

Amalie had the information she needed and even managed to get a ride to Stocksee. Could *Helga be here?* She asked herself.

The hospital where Helga Oppenheimer was supposedly working since her release was little more than a large house. When the enemy had been pushed back beyond the border during the war, they seized the house for their own purposes, flying in medical staff and supplies. Now, the once large bedrooms were wards, but the kitchen and dining room retained their original design.

'May I help you?' the receptionist asked.

'I'd like to see the doctor.'

'Do you have an appointment?'

'No.'

'There is a queue. If you wish to take a seat, Dr Oppenheimer will see to you as soon as she can.' The name sent a chill down Amalie's spine. The cold institutional floor and plain decorated walls were akin to a funeral home. The room smelled like urine, faeces, body odour, and disinfectant, but the most poignant smell was death.

An elderly lady walked towards Amalie, 'she'll want to strip wash you and look at your cowbells,' she stated and nodded before carrying on her journey.

The receptionist stood up and cleared her throat. 'Mags, I've told you before you must stay in your room and not bother the other patients.'

The old lady rolled her eyes and looked back at Amalie. 'She's a mermaid, and she's had sex with two doctors today already.'

'MAGS,' shouted the receptionist.

'God, you're fucking ugly. OK, I'm going.' The old lady gave a little wave to Amalie, and Amalie smiled.

The door to the consultation room opened and a familiar face emerged. 'WER KOMMT ALS NÄCHSTES?' *Who is next?* 'Mags, what are you doing out?' she asked sternly.

The receptionist hurried towards Mags to guide her back to her room. 'Sorry, Helga, she won't get out again.'

'Never mind! Mags, aren't you due another injection?' she asked sadistically.

'You just want to look at my arse again, don't you?' Mags answered as she walked inside. 'Go on then, one more look. But, you're not looking at my cowbells again although you'll be dead in the morning anyway.'

Helga had been too focused on the old lady to even acknowledge Amalie, but, would she recognise her after all these years anyway? Amalie's fears had been confirmed. She finally tracked down the woman who haunted her dreams that always included the shrill voices of the murdered children as the sharp blade stroked innocent skin.

Adrenaline flooded Amalie's system, pumping and beating like it wanted to escape. Her heart beat furiously and she wanted to run, run as fast as she could for the safety of the hills, but another part of her wanted to open a chest of weaponry. She tasted the saliva thickening in her mouth like a rabid dog, and beads of sweat formed on her brow. She waited patiently outside, waited for Dr Oppenheimer to go home. At some point, Amalie would have to make her move.

Helga took a perverse pleasure in attaining a position of trust and respect. She came across as charming and intelligent but she didn't play by the same rule book as the rest of society, and neither did Amalie. Amalie knew that if she didn't act, then *they,* these evolutionary throwbacks, would continue driving us into a fiendish dystopia and dominate our world. No one knew about Helga and who she was; how could they? Why would anyone want such an amoral, unscrupulous fiend on their doorstep? Something needed to be done.

CHAPTER 16

"Danger hides in beauty, and beauty in danger."
Belva Plain.

Amalie kept a constant stare from a seat outside a coffee house opposite Helga's clinic. Her gaze was unwavering and transfixed as her mark, Helga, made her appearance at the end of the day, locking the door to the clinic behind her. Amalie's eyes widened and followed Helga as if a cat was stalking a mouse. She stood up and melted into the darkness, and she followed Helga home. Helga's brown hair flowed down onto her shoulders falling in soft layers as she walked home. She even looked from side to side as if anxious someone was following her. Someone was. Amalie could tell Helga worked out; her physique was square and her shoulders broad, honed from hours and hours of bench presses and Amalie knew she wouldn't easily be overpowered. As agile as Amalie was, she knew she had to take the element of surprise as her method of restraint, she wanted to reach out and touch her, to feel her. Helga opened her front door and fell without even a whimper; unaware of her shortcoming. One minute she was planning a quiet night in and the next, bang ready for dispatch.

Helga's eyes opened, her naked body lay in the bathtub with rope binding her hands in front of her.

'Wer bist du?' *Who are you?* Helga asked.

'You know who I am.' Amalie answered.

'I think you have me mistaken,' Helga stated in

English with a heavy German accent.

'I don't think so...Helga...Oppenheimer, born 10th of May, 1912, in Cologne.'

'Do I know you?' she asked. Her *you* pronounced as zoo.

Amalie roared with laughter, *"Do you know me?"* You didn't care to know anyone...

Helga squinted her eyes to focus on Amalie.

'I don't just want to kill you,' Amalie said, 'I want to hear your cries, I want to witness the very second that you no longer exist.'

'I'm so, so, sorry,' Helga pleaded. Amalie grasped Helga's hair, her nails trailing her scalp as she pulled her head back and her lips turned upwards into a smile. Amalie stared into Helga's eyes for the fear she longed to see.

'You're that little bitch...' Helga realised. Amalie smiled at the pronunciation.

'There she is, good ole' Helga.'

'Are you going to kill me?'

'Yes.' Amalie answered.

'Look, what is that English expression? I think we started off on the wrong foot? I was just following orders,' Helga's voice changed to a panicking wail.

'And that's all you have is two wrong feet and fucking ugly shoes. I'm going to throw these out by the way. Now sit tight, I'll warm you up shortly.' Amalie reassured the German.

CHAPTER 17

*"Many men kill themselves for love, but many
more women die of it." Helen Rowland*

'DCI Owen, this is Steve Harrison - MI6.'

'Foreign intelligence?'

'Head of the European section. You'll be working alongside him from now on.'

'I'm not sure I understand what's going on here.'

'There's been a string of high profile murders across the United Kingdom.'

'But isn't MI6 involved in tracking and arresting assassins all over the world?'

'Exactly.'

The icy rain stabbed at Owen's eyes as he ran through it under the icy black sky after he met with MI6. It grumbled restlessly and the sky roared furiously as he headed for shelter in the car. The rain obscured Owen's vision and his flashlight died just feet away from the car. The water trickled freely down the sides of his face, and he began to try and drown out his attempt to soothe himself as it wouldn't do him any favours in front of his superiors.

The loud untamed thunder rattled the car whilst Owen caught his breath.

What a night!

The rain hammered onto the steel exterior, thundering like a drummer. Every driver on the road crawled at a snail's pace, visibility proved poor in the torrential rain, and Owen failed to compose himself after receiving news on his new assignment. His morbid interest in criminology had once been a fantasy, having read all the Bond novels to date. He dreamed of becoming a secret agent in the MI6 department like Bond, but in reality, roles like this were just in the movies. Owen signed up to protect and serve; maybe he was like his father – old fashioned? He was the type of man who would have rolled off the assembly line for FBI agents - A serious man, with no shades of grey. He put in more hours than any other officer, and if MI6 were looking to team up with a DCI – Owen was the man for the job.

Steve Harrison had hair akin to Humphrey Bogart in his pomp and a smile so white it could only be gazed upon with heavy-duty sunglasses like Titmus or Wayfarers. Owen could really imagine Harrison coming out with "here's looking at you kid," but not quite in the charming way Bogart managed.

He explained to Owen that they were to scan the area and pay special attention to thieves, rogues, and general vagabonds. But Owen wasn't with MI6 for that, and if he wanted that sort of lifestyle he would have stayed with the Stafford Police. It appeared that these lowlife criminals were queuing up for the opportunity to dispossess the locals of their goods and chattels. A stakeout for Owen meant a cold nine hours and an even colder coffee. Inevitably in the movies, the bad guy always showed up, there was a chase, the bad guy got caught, and the media had a field day. That day had already happened to Owen, he wasn't that lucky to get another win like that one. Harrison called it surveillance, and it passed like a bad dream. The boredom ate away at his brain cells every minute he sat in the police vehicle with just the radio chatter for companionship, but this was what he signed up for, to follow orders and uphold the law. He sat in his car, watching.

It had only been the next day that Owen was informed of the true meaning of his stakeout; Harrison was hoping to catch a glimpse of the killer.

The following day Owen was sent into another meeting with Steve Harrison and his associates.

'Owen, I'm glad you could join us. Please, sit.'

Agent Harrison stared at Owen furrowing his brows. Owen fumbled with his briefcase, dropped his pen and scraped his chair.

'Are...' Harrison started.

Owen cleared his throat.

'Are you comfortable?' Harrison asked.

'Yes, thank you,' Owen answered.

'This operation is strictly between these four walls,' Harrison cautioned.

'Tell me what we've got.'

'We believe she has been operating for several years across three countries.'

'I'm not following?'

'Please don't interrupt, Owen.'

The other agents gave Owen a look of dismay. His eyes darted from one agent to another taking in every word that Harrison spoke...

'She's highly skilled, and to be honest, she's starting to show off.'

Steve handed over a folder containing documents relevant to female multiple killers.

'I see. And you want me to...?' Owen questioned.

'Find her. What do you know about female

multiple killers, Owen?'

Owen was fascinated with crime, his fascination even bordered on obsession, and now here he is faced with an assassin that had brought the attention of MI6. *Who is she? How do we even know she is a she?*

'I....' Owen started.

'Spit it out, we haven't all day,' hissed Harrison as the other agents gawped.

'I'd say, unlike their male counterparts, their motives would differ significantly,' Owen countered.

'How so?'

'I would say sex would generally be further down the list of reasons why a woman would kill. Sexual and sadistic motives I have found are extremely rare and unheard of with female killers.'

'Interesting. What else?' Harrison nodded.

'Male multiple killers tend to be driven by sexual lust, and females more than likely kill for profit or revenge. Why do you think this person is female?'

'We didn't, but we do now.'

VI

LONDON, ENGLAND

CHAPTER 18

"Hell is empty and all the devils are here!"
William Shakespeare

The Kew Palace, with its red brick magnificence, stood proudly on the banks of the River Thames. The Georgian decor told the story of its wondrous historic beauty. The Palace's red coloured exterior looked as if was a dolls house sat among a wide variety of fauna. The sculptures, too, were exquisite, as was the Chinese Pagoda which was built in 1762. The Palace and its charming rooms were filled with inquisitive objects. The detailed library and top floor, almost untouched for two centuries, provided the perfect conference room for The Brotherhood.

At first, the men of around middle age looked innocuous enough. Their success was made obvious by their mannerisms and choice of attire. Their bland faces with no distinguishing features could not easily be remembered.

Their predatory focus was anything from ordinary, and the morning passed at a rapid rate in languages of English, French and Spanish – to accommodate all that were present.

The first man to speak, Charrière, was a clean-shaven man in his fifties. His sleek, combed back hair revealed his ageless and uniform skin. His eyes were dark, and he addressed his fellow members directly, with his cruel cold-hearted tone it assured their full attention. As a young man, he witnessed a massacre of villagers by German soldiers, and after the German defeat of France, French citizens were drafted into forced labour in Germany. He later claimed that during the period of German occupation in France, Charrière engaged in the development of secret weapons that killed Germans, was involved in high level allied meetings, and worked with a group of Spanish anti-fascists. Towards the end of WW2, neighbours of Charrière complained to police about a foul smell. Upon entering, they found human remains and enough parts to account for at least five victims. Personal items scattered around the property also belonged to his victims. A media frenzy ensued with newspapers titling him the Werewolf of Paris. He hid with friends until The National Gendarmerie closed in on him. He then fled to England and joined The Brotherhood.

After a few hours of economics and political affairs, their attention turned to a disturbing matter.

'Gentlemen it has been brought to my attention that one of our associates has been murdered. A witness places a young woman at the scene.'

He passed a photograph of the crime scene around the men sitting at the table. The deceased resembled a ghoul; his grey complexion contrasted the red arteries and blood that had seeped from the laceration to his abdomen. His innards had spilt like grey serpents, and his skin had stained from where police officers had found him in the sewers. He lay like a butchered animal. His skull smashed in and his mouth was open with a ball of fabric stuffed inside.

'Suspect?' A voice asked from beside the speaker.

'The suspect looked like anyone and no one. But

she's female.'

'Please no...' begged a fellow member that sat at the long table.

'If you can't control your dog, William, then we will do it for you,' Charrière snarled. His eyes were jet black and more fearsome than a lion. A match struck sandy paper and ignited the match instantly. It was brought to the lips of another member as he lighted a cigarette that hung from his lip. A cloud of smoke escaped the corner of his mouth as he watched William beg. The man's free hand lay loosely over a handgun beside him and his finger gently stroked the trigger.

'That won't be necessary,' Charrière said and redirected his question at William. 'Will it?'

William had to choose a side; with the Second World War over, choosing your side of whom to trust was ever more important, no one would ask a savage for help – not unless they were their only option. William had no interest in The Brotherhood's world of violence and hatred, and he knew children with more morals than the brainless wannabes here, but they had guns – William didn't – not here anyway. His eyes met theirs briefly; he gave a slight nod and lowered his head in acceptance. Only for so long could William contain himself, he never was a violent man but after each verbal beating, he was that much closer to an explosion. His anger began to churn, and he had to choose his words carefully – after all, he wasn't stroking the trigger. Rumour had it the numb knuckle that was sat beside him was known as "The Butcher" as he'd carve up his victims and hang them from meat hooks, but he was just some lap dog, throw him a bone and he would forget about his previous owner and become your new best friend.

William stood up, his eyes met Charrière's, no one got to be in Charrière's position without having the conscience and compassion of a cockroach. Charrière was the boss here; maybe it was his instinct for cruelty, his lack of morals that made the other members respect him? Or was it fear? Sure, Charrière scared William shitless! But, that feeling never made it to his facial muscles. He remained relaxed, his eyes transfixed to Charrière's. Showing a sign of weakness could be his undoing. William had spent years of masking his feelings and as he spoke his words were evenly spaced, clear, and concise.

'No, it won't be necessary, Charrière.'

'Good, now...' Charrière finished.

'I've not finished, Charrière,' William interrupted.

'Excusez-moi, William?'

'Sit down!' William stated matter-of-factly. William placed the photograph of the deceased onto the table. 'Looks like you've already made up your minds, but let me tell you something. If any harm comes to my niece, I will end you.'

'Are you threatening us?'

'Oh no, that would imply a possibility. I can assure you, this is a promise.'

The lapdog with the gun flinched and started to speak, 'Charrière?'

'Who gave you a speaking part?' William snapped as his brows rose. He knew there was only one way out alive for him and Amalie, and the only code worth following was to rule or be ruled – that's the way it was.

'Now gentlemen,' William's violence was in his words, 'I'm a kind person but please do not mistake my kindness for weakness. Now, I'm going to make you an offer, an offer you can't refuse. You see money talks and I have oodles of it. So tell me, what's your price?'

Charrière answered, 'She's a liability.'

'An asset in hiding I'd rather call it. Let me put it in simple terms, Lucky wouldn't like his favourite British Bambina going missing, would he?'

'You know Charles Luciano?' coughed the lap dog.

'Very well,' Charrière concluded.

Charles "Lucky" Luciano, known as the real-life Godfather of organised crime, was recruited into gangster life at an early age. After moving to the United States and settling in the Lower East Side he became a leading member of the deadly Five Points Gang in Manhattan and began dealing Heroin. Around the beginning of Prohibition in the 1920s, he was recruited by Giuseppe Masseria also known as "Joe the Boss" making Lucky his top Lieutenant, and a few years after that, he went to work for Arnold Rothstein; a Kingpin in the Prohibition era and a known loan shark and gambler. By the mid-'20s, Luciano was reportedly making millions in bootlegging profits.

Everyone in The Brotherhood had heard of Charles Luciano, and how he obtained his nickname "Lucky" and most famously how he miraculously survived a kidnapping by rivals where they beat him, slit his throat and stabbed him multiple times with an ice pick then left him for dead on New York's Staten

Island.

After a feud between two crime families; Maranzano and Masseria, Luciano formed connections with second-tier leaders and early on in 1931, in a secret deal with Maranzano, Luciano agreed to engineer the death of his boss, Masseria. In return, Luciano would receive Masseria's rackets and become Maranzano's second in command.

Maranzano became New York's *capo di tutti I Capi* "Boss of Bosses", but when Luciano learned that his new boss Maranzano had planned to have him murdered, he sent his own men to assassinate Maranzano. With him dead, Luciano became the top leader in the New York Mafia in late 1931. If Lord William was on friendly terms with Luciano, he was a respected man.

VII

PARIS, FRANCE

CHAPTER 19

Challenging me will be your last mistake.

It had been a fortnight since Amalie had seen Helga. At mid-morning, she sat at an outside table of a cosy coffee shop in the heart of Paris. Its bright pink facade, earthy interior, high ceiling, and exposed stone walls attracted a bountiful crowd. Most of the tables were occupied, and Amalie subtly observed her surroundings.

'Bonjour Madam, your cafe.'

'Merci.'

For a moment she felt normal, she smiled and laughed quietly to a couple's jokes then took another sip of her coffee. She wondered if the couple was married, lovers or related. There was tension between them. Her eyes darted from the man to the woman and back to the man. Rich, Amalie concluded. The woman's jewellery glistened, the bottle on the table – also expensive. Amalie admired her style, her hair, makeup and mannerisms, and Amalie tucked a stray curl of hair behind her ear. Amalie learned that the woman was a fashion designer, her male companion – a photographer. Neither were related nor showed any signs of an affair. Their erotic intimacy intrigued Amalie into how this particular couple had lured her into their bubble.

'Excusez-moi,' Amalie smiled as she walked towards their table.

'Oui?' they began.

'Parles-tu Anglais?'

'Yes. What can we do for you?' the woman asked.

'I'm ever so sorry to intrude, but I'm a little lost.'

The French couple invited Amalie for a drink, and she informed them of her make-believe existence and her top floor apartment overlooking the Eiffel Tower. Her cover story was executed to perfection as if she had recited it from a script in a play.

Of course, the couple had no reason to disbelieve her; Paris was the perfect location for Amalie to show off her recent Dior gifts from William. They seemed intrigued and loved her couture pieces. Of course, Amalie had the first choice of the latest trends thanks to her uncle. 'I must leave,' Amalie smiled and nodded before the couple could mutter another word.

A short drive took Amalie to her temporary accommodation – a 1930s building, quiet, and yes, some of her cover stories had been based on truth. It had wooden floorboards and silk drapes, but those were from the previous tenant. In reality, Amalie didn't care much for the finer things in life. The apartment offered little space compared to her uncle's stately home, but it was hers, for now. The apartment came fully furnished, and she had little interest in adding personal touches. She didn't know anyone, let alone have any guests or even know how long she was going to stay. Her professional dealings took place in public areas, and her sexual interests – if there were any, would be at motels. Private space was important to her; never again did she want to share a bunk, a soup bowl, or a slice of bread. But, one other thing was important to Amalie and that was her interest in the arts. Her small compact library would always ensure a small selection of Shakespearean plays and poems. But, Amalie was bored, she missed the stiff upper lip of her uncle and decided she'd keep her Parisian apartment but would return to England.

Amalie would recall her time at the orphanage, the food barely edible, the hygiene non-existent and the eerie winds and creaky floorboards that penetrated to the very bones of the children that resided inside. Their slightest infraction of the rules resulted in punishment. Amalie had been fortunate to have only been there a short while when she was requested to move to England.

When she returned from Paris, William was thrilled to see his niece well, and she confided in him about her time at the orphanage. He begged her again to stay, change her ways, make a new life and for a small amount of time she considered it, but a question gnawed at him.

'Did you go to Germany and find what you were looking for?'

'Yes,' she answered.

'What were you thinking? In fact, don't answer that! We have a problem.'

'Excuse me, Sir,' Mrs Campbell interrupted, 'someone is here to see you.'

'Let them in.'

The speaker from The Brotherhood, Charrière, walked into the room. William stood up and greeted him formally and walked out. His jet black eyes transfixed onto Amalie, and he sat without invitation.

He looked ordinary enough, but his piercing look told her that he wasn't someone she could manipulate.

'Amalie, Amalie, Amalie. What may we do with you?'

Her eyes were blank.

'It's just as well your uncle is here and I saw your photograph before the police found you, or we wouldn't be having this conversation now, would we?'

She glanced at him again not saying a word.

'All business then? Let me confirm your identity. Amalie Keller, twenty-four-years old. When you were ten years old, your father returned to the United Kingdom, and your mother, brother and yourself were captured by the SS?'

'What do you want?'

'I have your case file here from the orphanage; it states you did not interact much with the other children? The orphanage also failed to inform your uncle of your sociopathic behavioural pattern. Despite all of this, your uncle informs me that your homeschooling has received exceptional results and your ability for languages and the arts has been praised on more than one occasion by your tutors, and yet you don't leave the house? Do you have no friends? You have however formed a deep emotional attachment to your uncle.'

'Is that a crime?'

'Not at all, only, you *have* left the house, haven't you?'

'Is this going somewhere? I have another engagement,' Amalie said as she stood up.

'You won't be going anywhere. Sit down!'

'What do you want?'

'Just a chat. Rumour has it you were in Stocksee;

bring back old memories did it? Not quite the behaviour I'd expect from an exceptional academic student, would you agree?'

She looked away, unable to answer.

'It was an effective job – who taught you?'

'Excuse me?'

'Concentrated sulphuric acid – genius.'

'You have me mistaken for someone else.'

'I doubt that very much. Of course, it is perfectly understandable – you being the last remaining survivor of your *other* family.'

'You came all this way to talk all about little me?'

'No, what you did to that sausage-eating-bitch does not concern me, but I'm here on another matter. A matter of which a witness placed you at a scene stating you were extremely agitated when approached by local stallholders when they subjected you to verbal assault. It just so happens a month later, he, help me here, what's the English expression? Pops up dead?'

'Who?'

'The man at the market of course.'

'Hmm that's a shame,' she stated unsympathetically.

'Tell me, Amalie, what did it feel like?'

Her expression was blank. 'Hypothetically of course, as you clearly have no idea what I'm talking about,' he humoured her.

'Hypothetically I may have felt a sense of satisfaction – he was a pig.'

'Yes, he was, in fact, that's why I hired him. And now, how do you feel?'

'Nothing.'

'So, after you have rid the world of your adversaries, then what... life imprisonment?'

'Your point is?'

William walked back into the room. 'This is going nowhere.'

'The truth is, Amalie, "one kills a man, one is an assassin; one kills millions, one is a conqueror, one kills everybody, one is God".'

'Don't get carried away with yourself.'

'What I'm trying to tell you, Amalie, is in life there has to be a balance. Take Colonel Claus von Stauffenberg for instance.'

'I'm sorry, who?'

'Many German officers knew they were going to lose the war and an honourable surrender would be their only way out. However, they knew they would have to eliminate their greatest obstacle, Adolf Hitler.'

'There were *many* attempts on Hitler's life.'

'All had failed. The leader, Colonel Stauffenberg led an operation to assassinate and create a political coup as a desperate measure against Hitler. They planned to place a bomb in Der Führer's bunker known as the Wolf's Lair and return to Berlin to take charge of the operation.'

'Hitler never went anywhere without his ring of steel.'

'Precisely! So Stauffenberg's operation Valkyrie included rounding up the SS.'

'And you brought me here to reminisce about one of the world's most horrific events?'

'No, Amalie. I want to employ you. What I'm trying to say to you is, it failed because a man called

Otto Skorzeny managed to infiltrate the conspirator's base of operations and managed to get the Valkyrie order rescinded. He intended to quell the possible coup that had been set up to trick German troops into arresting loyal Nazi officials.'

'It was Skorzeny's actions that contributed to the restoration of communications to the Fuhrer?'

'Yes. So, you've always got to have a plan B.'

'And I'm your plan B?' she nodded.

'Correct,' he laughed.

There was a long silence. She stared through the window pane out onto the mowed lawn.

'I'm doing just fine on my own.'

'Let me make this clear. You will.' Everything in Amalie's life had been waiting for this moment. It was as if her life suddenly had meaning to it. Her eyes began to dry where she didn't blink, she reached for her tea, 'Well, you've not given me much choice have you?'

CHAPTER 20

You're a soldier now

Amalie reminisced about her last words with Charrière.

'You're young and you're dumb Amalie.'

'Then teach me.'

Those were the last words from Charrière as he left. Never had Amalie thought of herself as dumb!

William stood in front of Amalie with his gun in his hand; it was pointed at the floor with the safety on. Amalie's heart started racing but she never feared what might happen. The metal barrel glistened brightly, and she heard a click as he switched the safety off. Amalie's mouth curved upwards, she smiled like a child opening Christmas presents, her eyes were fiery, and she reached forward to take it from his hand.

'NO!'

The adrenaline coursed through her veins. The last time she had laid eyes on such a clunk of metal had been at Auschwitz in the hands of the Schutzstaffel, and she longed to feel its power. She tried to breathe in and out and could feel her pulse beating and her hands full of sweat.

'I'm just showing you, Amalie. You are never to use it. To use a gun for malice is like losing part of your soul.'

'Then why do *you* have it?'

'For protection, you can never be too careful these

days. I just want you to remember that before Charrière starts.'

Over the next few months, Amalie learned everything from self-defence to anti-terrorism tactics. She perversely enjoyed her transformation, but the first days were the worst.

She recalled the door opening slowly and Charrière emerged behind it.

'Bonjour, Mademoiselle,' he announced in his usual thick French accent.

'Good morning.'

He stood there smirking as he looked Amalie up and down, the arrogance in his triumph expelled through his laughter as several men walked in, whipped a black hood over Amalie's head and shoved her into the back of a car.

She wanted to run but she knew she hadn't come this far to flee just yet.

Centuries later, after the Romans used it as a cavalry base, central Brecon Beacons soon became an iconic place of importance for military use. Rifle butts in Cwm Llwch provided evidence dating as far back as the 19th century.

On arrival, Amalie's hood was removed. She had no idea where she was, and Charrière was talking to another man just out of earshot. She jerked and panicked. Her wrists were bound behind her, and something sharp sliced into her skin.

'Well what do we 'av 'ere, Charrière? Looks like fine country pussy.'

'Amalie, this is Glen Carter, he will be taking care of you until I return.'

Carter's savage eyes disappeared deeper into his thick skull. His face contorted with a burning hatred as he cracked his knuckles within the palm of his other hand. His SAS days were over and he had little time for a skinny wafer like Amalie. All he knew was he had to keep her alive but have her ready in three months.

'I want her back in three months, Carter.'

'Ya 'avin' a laugh ain't ya. Six minimum, mind you a scrawny chicken leg like this won't last a day.'

'Three months - alive!'

Carter groaned. He worked at the training camp and live firing range in Cwn Gwdi and had a no-bullshit attitude. Charrière had told her Carter was involved in the Small Scale Raiding Force (SSRF) of the 40s. At the time, Churchill believed that the raids against the German defences in occupied France would have a demoralising effect on the German troops. Those that were selected for SSRF were trained in Commando style combat, and Carter was built like a brick shit house.

Amalie was sent to a special selection process. It began with three weeks of endurance marches in the British countryside and designed to push her mental and physical stamina to the limit.

The first day was the hardest, keeping warm was her first challenge. With her Bergen filled with bricks, Amalie convulsed at the exhaustion. Carter screamed at the slightest thing, and it made her quake when she heard it. She felt like creeping into his hut in the middle of the night and slicing through his jugular, but in reality, by 8 pm she was dead to the world. Every day the distance grew further and the burden became heavier. She'd look into his empty eyes, devoid of life.

'Stop eyeballing me, Sprog, you're up here with all the other lost souls and there's nawt ya can do 'bout it,' he would growl.

She turned her eyes away for a moment, his skin was taught over rounded muscles. The instructor was always shouting, telling her off, asking if she wanted to quit but being told off became a privilege – being ignored would have been far worse.

'You know what happened to the last boy that eyeballed me, kid? He died and the ravens gripped his lids while they had his eyes for breakfast.'

Every day she was roused from her sleep, kicked out from beneath her blanket and forced into clothing that didn't fit, boots that didn't do up. She was thrown into a truck and dumped in the middle of nowhere and expected to return within a certain time frame. Scent dogs would howl in the distance looking for her, and she learned the hard way asking a local for directions. They, of course, reported back to Carter, and Amalie was punished by having her head held in a bucket of icy water. To stave off hunger, she would gather bird's eggs to cook over a small campfire, and she would lick at leaves during the morning dew to quench her thirst. Within just a few days Carter had managed to systematically chastise and humiliate her.

'Move it! MOVE, MOVE, MOVE! Ready to quit yet?' he yelled, 'CHECKPOINT!'

Weapons training was sporadic, Amalie was stopped at a checkpoint, Carter weighed her Bergen,

'41lbs,' he mumbled. He handed her an AK47. 'Strip it, tell me how it works.'

Amalie never hated anyone, not since her liberation, and William tried to teach her that hate was a sin, there was always a temptation to follow its path without logic and reason, and it only brought pain and suffering. It would show your shame and insecurities. It was far easier to act out in the name of hate and cast yourself as a victim in your own play. But, she hated Carter, that she knew for sure. Determination kept her going, to prove to Charrière she wasn't a dumb fine country pussy but an elite warrior.

As if the assault course hadn't been enough, she endured the Brecon mile complete with the rifle in tow. It wasn't a pass or fail type of course, but Amalie's alternatives were 10ft below ground. She doubled over, soaking and freezing from exhaustion. Carter wasn't concerned that she changed out of her wet clothing, drank water or caught her breath – he had a job to do. Sure he had to keep her alive, but that's where it ended.

The ground was sodden and slippery. It had rained for days, and as the instructor looked on, Amalie began occupying harbour – displaying a defensive formation for her platoon. Of course, she was alone and rolled her eyes at her pretend teammates.

'This is ridiculous,' she murmured.

'What, what did you say? I didn't ask you to speak, Sprog!'

'There is no one here.'

'I don't give a shit. I want to make sure ya can get yourself out of a killing area.'

Three months of training was coming to an end and Carter kicked Amalie out of bed for the last time. He swung at her with a fast forward kick to the ribs, and she howled in agony. She got to her feet, raced towards him, and struck him in his jaw. He spat out a few teeth, and blood appeared from his nose and gum. She grabbed his wrist, twisted it behind him, and forced his head into the ice bucket whilst straddling his shoulders. He convulsed as he took in water.

'Who's fine country pussy now?' She gritted her teeth. As much as she wanted to kill him, she needed him. Someone had to witness how far she had come.

'Enough?'

A gurgle emerged from the water, and Amalie pulled his head up and stared into his eyes. He nodded and she let him go.

The next day had been her first morning without being kicked out of bed. Charrière furrowed his brows at Carter. 'Did you play nice?' he said glancing at Amalie.

'Ah mon chéri, Amalie, look at you. Carter, is my budding cherry ready?'

'If a kook is what ya after!' Carter answered.

'It's easy to label people names in this world we live in, Carter. We all go a little crazy sometimes.'

'She's unpredictable' Carter pointed.

'Exactly, a job well done. Amalie, we're leaving.' Charrière demanded.

Amalie followed Charrière to the car. Carter looked on in amusement.

'Carter,' she whispered, 'call me a kook again and you might find that double-edged commando knife you keep beside you at night thrust into one of your balls. I'm sure it would slice like a knife through butter.'

CHAPTER 21

Because no one else can

The people of Britain were still grieving from the London smog that lasted five days and killed more than four thousand people from heart and lung disease-related illnesses. Environmental pollution was the price Britain paid for industrial success, and in industrialised areas, the factories not only polluted the air but also the water, and mines tarred the landscape. Britain became the foremost producer of ships and leading producer of coal, steel, textiles, and cars. Yet with success came failure, and many country residents still lacked modern facilities. It encouraged hostility and often resulted in violence. In 1952, the river at Lynmouth flooded and led to more deaths. William wasn't his usual self – he tucked himself away in his study for hours at a time. Amalie was worried, but he snapped if she asked after his well being so she spent her time reading up on some of her favourite plays.

Charrière had promised to be in touch through the Obituary section of the Daily Mirror but it had been four weeks since he collected her from Carter and his lecture on how she would proceed as they returned to Surrey.

That evening, the city's light began to fade and Amalie opened her copy of the Daily Mirror. In the Obituary, it read:

Bonacci, James, of 615, London, passed peacefully

at home. He was a loving faithful husband of 60 years to Judy Taylor who preceded his death. They will be dearly missed by their daughter of 24.

Amalie recognised the series of numbers from the local library; 615 represented the shelf range and within each bay of shelves, code numbers were ordered from left to right descending in a zigzag formation. Next, she would examine each shelf by level then by the bay to find 615 first. The third bay displayed 615...her eyes darted from one book to another looking for the next numbers in the sequence. Bingo, last level. Inside the book, *King Lear* was a white envelope and a photograph of a middle-aged man. A man, a man she did not recognise, and a message scribbled on the back. *It must be from Charrière!*

1-19-19-9-7-14-13-5-14-20

"13-1-4" 6-18-1-14-11-9-5 6-1-2-15-26-26-9

At first glance, the numbers looked completely random. Amalie had become accustomed to symbology through the expression of creativity in literature and the performing arts. But, if Charrière was trying to send some sort of message, at this point Amalie had no idea what it meant. She tucked the envelope into her pocket, looked over her shoulder and exited the library.

It didn't take Amalie long to work out that "Mad" Frankie Fabozzi was her target. Amalie refrained from knowing who Mad Frankie was, she preferred

not to think of them at all and if she did, it was
thinking as if they were already dead. To Amalie, it
was a job, everyone has to die at some point, and she
considered it a great way to go. No goodbyes, no
illnesses and suffering. One minute they're minding
their own business, and the next, gone, dispatched,
painless; unless the subject was one of Amalie's
targets, of course.

Amalie sipped on her espresso, pursing her red lips
to the edge of the cup. She had barely drank anything
when her subject Frankie Fabozzi walked in. *Damn.
He's early.* She contemplated charging extra for
having to leave a perfectly decent cup of coffee, and
it upset her morals to leave the drink behind. She
smiled coyly as he gazed at her for a moment before
ordering a Scotch. Her playful eyes and vivacious
smile offered him no inclination of his fate that lay
ahead. She inhaled deeply as she stood, gathered her
handbag, adjusted her dress and she swept her blonde
wig back away from her face. She removed the vial of
poison inside a hairpin and tucked it into the palm of
her hand as she strolled towards her target. In the
final seconds, she looked into his eyes, she smiled
and he knew at that very moment something was
amiss. As she brushed past him on her way out of the
coffee house, the vial pierced his hip like a
hypodermic needle, injecting the potassium cyanide.
'Oh do forgive me!' She apologetically smiled and
then she walked away.

Amalie never looked back, even while he struggled
to catch his breath, inhaling deeply. He never felt his
collision with the ground. Panic rose and everyone

screamed. Amalie shook her head, annoyed at herself that she couldn't whack someone off without looking at them in the eye. *Always room for improvement.*

CHAPTER 22

Look me in the eyes when I stare at you

Owen placed the key in the lock to his front door. It creaked open the same as it did the day before and the day before that. He threw his briefcase on the couch and made his way to his bedroom. The house was empty, there was no sign of a family. He never married as he had never wanted to have his wife go through the trauma that his mother did when his father died in the line of duty. His colleagues mocked him for his clean looks, and his dark hair was closely cropped to perfection. Part of his morning routine included a shave with a cut-throat razor, and afterwards he would feel his skin across his jaw to test its smoothness. He had the kind of face that would turn heads, and despite the opportunities that came his way, he wasn't attracted to high heels and lipstick. She had to be able to have an intelligent conversation.

Owen was as stiff as his suit, and conversation with him during work hours was as interesting as watching paint dry but he noticed things other people didn't. He just listened, watched their eye movements and body language, and then he'd come out with a perfect one-liner like he genuinely wanted to know. It led to many leads and during an investigation; you could rely on Owen to notice anything peculiar. Nothing was inconsequential if it was work-related, but a creeping sense of dissatisfaction would gnaw at him on the lonely evenings. In reality, he looked for trouble to combat boredom. He wanted it all, the action, rule-breaking, even the bloodshed, and up to now his glorified idea of a career had been nothing but a fantasy.

Owen had previously been at the MI6 meeting with Steve Harrison as he informed the team of the assassination of Helga Oppenheimer. That evening, Harrison had given Owen a folder of documents to read on the subject of Femme Fatales and wanted his opinions the following day.

Owen asked another member in MI6 to look up any females worldwide that have any medical or prison records that would display any psychopathic traits and requested he be informed immediately of any leads.

As he flicked the switch to his bedroom, the light adorned the wall at the end of his bed. His eyes scanned from one end to another, gazing over years of research. He removed one of the documents and taped it to the wall stroking his finger over the black and white photo; the blurred image of a woman's face.

The following day it was noted that the investigation was temporarily on hold. The British public reacted with consternation after it was revealed that MI6 had been infiltrated by Soviet double agents since the '30s. From then on, any information of MI6 operations seldom appeared in the British press.

'I want this kept under wraps, you hear me?' Harrison stated. 'We can't afford another cock-up and risk losing everything we've worked on here.'

'What about this operation?' another agent asked.

'We carry on. Who's got news? Owen?' Harrison asked.

'I believe we have an assassin,' Owen answered.

'No shit, Sherlock.'

'No pattern, no face.'

'She can't be running this shit show alone?' Harrison questioned.

'We find her, we find *them*.'

Steve Harrison walked out of the room and an agent leaned across to Owen, 'Welcome to MI6,' Morley greeted Owen. 'I wonder what you have to offer this department.'

'I beg your pardon?'

'Well, I'm not so sure you're cut out for this type of thing.'

'And what kind of *thing* would you be referring to?'

'Take this case last week; suspicious death? A man was found dead in a washing machine. The residence was secured, even bed sheets and water were found in the machine, but his head was not in the water. Any idea what could have happened?' Morley asked smugly.

'Sounds like a simple case of autoerotic asphyxiation to me,' Owen shrugged.

'Excuse me?' Morley laughed nervously looking at his fellow agents.

'An atypical method of autoerotic asphyxiation; he climbed in headfirst, became stuck and died from positional asphyxia. Autoerotic deaths stress the importance of doing a thorough scene investigation. However, you did say the residence was secure. But, hell what do I know? I'm just a DCI.'

Steve Harrison walked in just as Owen had finished, and Harrison tapped him on the shoulder. 'Take no notice of Morley, Owen, you'll do fine, and correct, the coroner confirmed he suffocated.'

'Tell me, Owen,' Morley asked again, 'how much of the day do you spend thinking about her, this assassin?'

'Why does it matter?'

'Shit, Owen, you're only here because of your intuition. There's something you're not letting on.'

'Yeah, your breath stinks.'

DCI Owen stood from the table and gathered his belongings. Harrison was in the hallway speaking to his assistant. 'Will that be all Harrison?' Harrison nodded a sign of approval, and Owen glanced over his shoulder to make sure he wasn't being followed. As he entered another room his old friend Paul looked above his glasses, 'Owen, old buddy, how the bloody hell are you?' he piped.

'Good, look I need a favour,' Owen answered as he brought his forefinger to his lips, 'Shush.'

'Anything, old chap.' Paul offered.

'I need a sketch.'

'Let me grab a pen and paper. What am I drawing?'

'I can't really say – just trust me on this one?'

'You know me, mum's the word!' Paul nodded in compliance.

Owen described the woman from the photograph, 'delicate features, and large eyes – wide – alert with smooth clear skin and long loose dark hair.'

'What about her lips?'

What about her lips? The photo didn't reveal much

but he answered, 'full.'

'Sounds like the woman of my dreams,' Paul laughed. His freehand sketch rapidly revealed the image of a young woman. Owen glanced at the sheet of paper, taking it from Paul. 'Here you go, Sir.'

Owen folded the paper small enough to slip into his suit pocket. In the privacy of the bathroom, he withdrew the paper, opening it carefully. He examined the fine shades of Paul's pencil strokes, admiring the strand of hair that cascaded past her eye. He stroked her cheek carefully as to not smudge Paul's work and whispered, 'Who are you?'

VIII

PARIS, FRANCE

CHAPTER 23

"She's mad but she's magic. There's no lie in her fire." Charles Bukowski

Amalie's recruitment by The Brotherhood had become a flawlessly executed plan. She did as she was told, and her murders were well performed. Carter's training had removed any guilt or conscience that remained, and she was highly praised. Her innocence and ability to transform into a somewhat normal human being hid her cold, soulless heart. But Amalie was playful, and she needed stimulation. Charrière had been displeased when she took unnecessary risks in creative murder techniques.

'*Putain* Amalie!' he shouted, 'In and out.'

'But…'

'No buts. You are attracting suspicion!'

Amalie was essentially still a child. She yearned to play again, buy fancy clothing, and be the budding niece that William had intended.

She ran a finger down the metal barrel of the gun and the anticipation of the bullet leaving her weapon sent a shiver down her spine. Her target stopped screaming momentarily.

'Is Cedar Smith your real name?' Amalie crinkled her nose looking at her distressed target.

'No, that's not me! You have me mistaken,' he wailed.

'I don't think so.' Cedar Smith was not his real

name, and Amalie cared less to find out. His hair was brown and greasy and he looked around forty-years old. Amalie didn't need to know his name; all she was concerned about was making sure her mark was dispatched so she would receive her pay. His photograph hadn't done him justice at all.

'Please, please...'

'Oh do shut up,' she answered, yawning whilst looking at her watch.

'Are you going to kill me?'

'Yes.'

'Oh dear God,' he prayed.

'God won't help you now.' Amalie rolled her eyes.

Her target started wailing again and Amalie sighed. She walked towards him placing the gun under his jaw, 'Is everything all right? You look a little pale. Maybe you need an iron supplement?'

Charrière's words entered her mind *"and stop playing with them".*

Why was a gun called a "piece"? After all, it brought anything but. Did Amalie ever have "peace" of mind by blowing someone else's? As the bullet left the barrel it spun its victim sideways propelling him backwards and, for a few seconds, his eyes widened as if he just hit a high for the last time.

Before the blood had congealed on his forehead, she was gone. She had been surprised at how little effort it took to dispatch him. The slight squeeze of the trigger and he was meat on the floor. It was harder cracking a walnut.

Amalie's next assignment took her to Paris. She walked through her apartment door with glee. The musty smell had been just as she had left it.

This time the target had been a name she recognised; a narcissistic pervert running the *Milieu corso-marseillais* in Paris. She had been ready with her knife. This one, she wanted to suffer. She entered the room of the *Hôtel de passé*.

After a successful campaign by a former prostitute, many of France's brothels aka *Maisons*, closed by 1946, so prostitution had become less visible and preserved the country's "public morality". However, former brothel owners refused to adhere to the new regulation and rebranded themselves, thus effectively making prostitution legal. Her target was a regular and it just so happened he enjoyed a young British filly.

Once the door slammed behind him, she tucked her knife beneath the pillow. Typically he disrespected women and liked to play rough, and he instructed her to fight back *"just a little"*.

As he started to straddle her, the cold steel penetrated his stomach. As she looked into his eyes, she smiled and twisted the blade further into his fleshy mound.

'You've got two potatoes but I can't see your parsnip? Is that British enough?'

He rolled over to his side, groaning and gurgling in agony as the crimson liquid spilt onto the bed sheets.

Charrière was waiting at the apartment when Amalie returned.

'Well?' he questioned.

'Well, what?'

'Is it done?'

'You always doubt me!' Amalie removed her clothes and sauntered into her bedroom. Charrière looked at her naked physique from top to bottom and shouted, 'Can you blame me?'

'What do you want from me, Charrière? *Oui* Sir, *non*, Sir?' She wrapped a silk negligee around her and brushed past him towards the kitchen.

'One target, that's all I asked.'

'Pardon my French, Charrière...but I'm bored.'

'I told you to stop playing with the targets,' he grunted.

'I didn't play with it, I chopped it off.'

'That wasn't part of the agreement.'

'Slip of the hand? If you're going to undermine me all the time, perhaps you need to hire a new recruit?' she shrugged.

'MI6 are all over this.'

'Are you worried?' Amalie laughed.

'Should I be?'

'I'm not. Relax. Dance with me, we're going to celebrate.'

'What's the occasion?'

'Do we need one?'

CHAPTER 24

"There is no beauty without some strangeness".
Edgar Allan Poe

The overcrowded slums that were built around 1864 in Paris were a maze of blind alleyways, passageways and workshops in unsanitary conditions. Children played in a site near the Renault car manufacturer west of central Paris, and Amalie found herself running through the streets at night to avoid large crowds of Parisians wallowing in misery. After the war, Paris's industry was ruined. Housing had been in short supply, and the city underwent major reconstruction with additional highways, skyscrapers, and thousands of new apartment blocks.

Another tenant two doors down had spotted Amalie and knocked on her apartment door.

'Hello?' she answered.

'Bonjour,' he said in a French accent. 'I noticed you're new around here? My name is Paul Miller.

'That doesn't sound very French.'

Miller was an assistant photographer on a three-month tour around Europe where he took photographs of celebrities including Christian Dior and Pablo Picasso. He was currently stationed in Paris and using his military pay to purchase equipment. Amalie found him amusing in that he used disguises to allow him to move through the streets without drawing attention from the locals. The Parisians knew all too well where ex-military men were headed – the pleasure houses. Amalie laughed at his jokes and his hunt for something worth capturing on his 35mm. "I knew when I took a good one," he would say, "for my body tingled and goosebumps popped up". Amalie could relate to that.

Every day in Paris, she'd start her day the same as the day before; a coffee and croissant on the Champs-Élysées in view of the *Arc de Triomphe*. This time she woke up in Paul's apartment to him opening the shutter that looked out onto his terrace.

'Good morning,' he smiled.

'Good morning.'

'I hope to see you later? I'm hoping to head towards the Louvre today.'

As Amalie dressed, she remembered Charrière. She could hear him talking to the landlady in the hallway about her whereabouts, and before long a pounding sounded at the door.

'Could you get that,' Paul bellowed from the bathroom.

As she answered the door, Charrière's expression worsened. 'What do you call this?'

'A bit of fun?' she shrugged.

'Get rid of it.'

'No.' She sulked.

'Get rid of it, or I will,' he demanded.

'But....'

'Amalie, I will wait down the hall.'

Amalie closed the door. Her hair hung loosely over her pale skin and as she walked towards the bathroom her hair swayed. Her eyes glistened as she took a knife out of the kitchen drawer. This kill was a means of necessity; she wouldn't lose a wink of sleep over it even if it had come earlier than she wanted. As Paul massaged the shampoo into his hair, the blade sliced across his throat. For a moment, she was lost. Her eyes narrowed, she didn't want to kill Paul – his skin felt so warm when he touched her and for a brief moment she felt normal.

This time she wanted him to die quickly; he wasn't a dirty, filthy scumbag, and she wasn't bored of him just yet.

'I have another job for you. But I don't want him dead.' Charrière stated.

'Can't it wait?'

'No. A Detective Chief Inspector is leading a department in London, just to find you.'

'What's his name?'

'DCI John Owen.'

'DCI? When did we start babysitting cops?'

'When did you start asking questions? Be subtle.'

'I can do subtle. D C I John Owen,' the name rolled off her tongue.

'Find out what they know, and put some clothes on for heaven's sake.'

'Oui, Monsieur,' she saluted.

IX

LONDON, ENGLAND

CHAPTER 25

*"Of all human weakness obsession is the most
dangerous" Woody Allen*

Another meeting with the rest of the MI6 team
exposed Helga Oppenheimer as a war criminal. The
coroner's report revealed no sign of sexual assault,
but she was alive when her skin started to dissolve. It
was clearly an act of revenge. It added more
corroboration to Owen's theory that they were
dealing with a woman.

Owen yearned for more. He wanted to be hands-
on; he wanted to see where *she* was. What else did he
have? With Harrison, it was all by the book. Owen
had to tread carefully around him. If he wasn't
careful, he'd have Owen's badge. Harrison's face was
as pliable as a piece of 4x2 and when he spoke, Owen
could hear the ex-military tone in his voice. He stood
like a mannequin and stank of cologne, and once he
had made up his mind that was it. Perhaps that's how
it was in MI6? He'd quick-draw faster than you could
blink, and you'd have to massage your hand to re-
circulate the blood if he ever shook it. The first sniff
of insubordination when you're on Harrison's team
you can kiss your career goodbye. Owen had been a
great choice, he knew the area, and he knew the
people. He had a good sixth sense and he knew what
rules he could bend –where and how far. Harrison
was a "Yes, Sir, No, Sir, three bags full, Sir" kind of
guy, and it was great working among all the

testosterone. But the thorn in Owen's side didn't go away.

'I'm not particularly interested in how this woman became a killer, Owen.'

'Well I am,' Owen answered, exacerbated.

'Why?'

'Because it's an itch I can't scratch, and it's disturbing my sleep.'

A knock at the door interrupted the conversation. The agents were informed another body had been found.

'Poison is an invisible murder weapon, Harrison. That's what makes it so appealing.'

'When did you become an expert?' coughed Agent Morley.

'Not an expert, but, in classical theatre, poison was always viewed as a woman's weapon.'

The other agents started laughing.

'IS SOMETHING AMUSING?' Harrison snapped.

'No, Sir...just...Didn't realise we had our very own Shakespeare here.'

'It's nothing to be amused at, Morley, nothing was too noisome for Shakespeare; he often used poisons as a weapon of choice for many of his iconic characters.' Harrison answered.

'Thank you, Harrison.'

CHAPTER 26

"I guess sometimes the past just catches up to you,
whether you want it to or not".
Dabbs Greer

Amalie just wanted revenge, it wasn't about counting
scalps. It was making sure everyone knew who these
bastards were. England hadn't been considered
necessarily a Nazi haven, but a few were living in
hiding.

The capture of Adolf Eichmann by a team of
Mossad operatives that made it their mission to bring
Nazi fugitives to justice had made newspaper
headlines. After ninety-nine holocaust survivors gave
evidence, Eichmann was found guilty of crimes
against humanity and being a member of a criminal
hostile organisation. Amalie sighed as she read the
article; Eichmann was one of the lucky ones; if she
had found him, he wouldn't be rotting in jail. It was
common knowledge that several survivors of the
holocaust including now minor celebrity Simon
Wiesenthal, dedicated their lives to finding Nazis.

Simon Wiesenthal was a Jewish Austrian
Holocaust survivor, and rumour had it he dedicated
his life to tracking down fugitive Nazis so that they
could be brought to trial. It's said he will soon be
opening a Documentation Centre of the Association
of Jewish Victims of the Nazi regime in Vienna, and
he *had* played a small role in the capture of
Eichmann.

It's not uncommon for Nazi war criminals to have already slipped into a grave before they could be placed in a courtroom. Former Nazi SS officers were found hanged by apparent suicides years after the end of the war, discovered in ditches at the side of the road; victims of so-called hit and runs. One was found in a hospital bed with kerosene in his bloodstream as he waited for minor surgery.

Wiesenthal without a doubt was soon on the rise to becoming one of the most famous Nazi hunters the world would ever see. A survivor of Mauthausen, he began to dedicate his life in the war crimes section of the United States Army gathering evidence to convict German war criminals. He wasn't about to let anyone who had committed the crimes against humanity just walk away.

Another such man was called Hanns Alexander. Although Alexander was born in Germany during World War 1 into an assimilated wealthy household, his Jewish family had fled to Britain when Hitler's rise to power threatened his family. His father was a popular doctor who was known to hold elaborate parties for the social elite including Albert Einstein. After the war ended, Alexander was one of the first volunteers wanting to investigate war-related crimes. A deep-seated rage fuelled his interest, and he'd drive around Europe with a dead Nazi strapped to his car. Amalie smiled as she recalled the memory when she read about his mission, she felt it far more interesting than the capture of Rudolf Höss; the exact details are unknown but he was either beaten by Jewish soldiers or forced to walk naked along a snowy road. However his fate ended, it wasn't enough, and later he was taken into custody and hanged a short while later.

William looked into Amalie's eyes. 'What will you do when you have completed your quota?'

'Well, I'll never be out of business, will I? I'm sure The Brotherhood will make sure of that.'

'And when all the criminals are captured?'

'We're all criminals in our own way.'

'When they are all dead?'

'I don't know, maybe I'll start playing the piano again.'

'Amalie, I'm being serious! Where will your role as this stubborn sleuth on the trail of the world's archfiends get you?'

'Uncle, what I do and others like me intend to do is keep a spotlight on this horrendous crime. Soon if we aren't careful, the world is disposed to forget.'

'Did you hear Otto Skorzeny is now over in Ireland?' Skorzeny was a name she had heard before.

Hitler's favourite Nazi commando Otto Skorzeny had arrived in Ireland in 1959. He was rumoured to be 6ft 4 and 18 stone. A distinctive scar on his left cheek that he received while fencing gave him the nickname "Scarface". Irish press described him as a glamorous cloak and dagger figure that everyone easily recognised in his local town, and the newspaper tone depicted more admiration than repulsion. It reported he had famously led the mission dubbed "Operation Oak" to rescue Hitler's ally, Benito Mussolini, when Mussolini was imprisoned in Italy at a villa on the Isle of La Maddalena near Sardinia. Winston Churchill, despite being an enemy of Skorzeny, once described the surprise attack on the Italian guards as "one of great daring".

Skorzeny had flown over in a Heinkel He-111 bomber and took aerial photos of the location, was then shot down by Allied soldiers, and crashed into the sea. Skorzeny and his men were rescued by an Italian warship, and he lost trace of Mussolini. But the defence didn't alter Skorzeny's determination, and finally, Mussolini was traced to a hotel in a remote resort on a mountain in central Italy.

Skorzeny received international stardom when he was seen at Mussolini's side being paraded in front of the media on the 12th of September, 1943. He was awarded the Knights cross by the Fuhrer for bravery and dubbed The Most Dangerous Man in Europe.

Amalie became interested in Skorzeny when she heard about one of his missions that apparently included the capture of Hungarian Admiral Horthy. He then rolled the Admiral in a carpet and sent him to Berlin.

But 10 days after Hitler claimed his own life, Skorzeny is said to have surrendered to the Americans. During the war trials, he was tried for violation of the laws of war in Dachau in 1947. The case collapsed, and Skorzeny was acquitted.

In July, 1948, he escaped with the help of former SS members who had dressed in US Military Police uniforms, entered the camp, and claimed they had been ordered to take Skorzeny to Nuremberg for a legal hearing.

His new business venture in Madrid became a front for organising the escape of wanted Nazis from Europe to South America, and his travels to Ireland came with a welcome reception from then Prime Minister Charles Haughey. It was this welcome invitation that may have encouraged Skorzeny to then purchase his 160-acre farm in County Kildare.

The local people applauded the presence of Skorzeny claiming that they would see this 6'4" giant driving a white Mercedes, visiting their stores, but he wasn't particularly friendly and didn't want to integrate.

Newspapers reported in the 1960s, that Skorzeny had created an escape path for Nazis in Spain with a secret organisation called Die Spinne, *The Spider*, that ended with some escaping to his farm in Ireland. That farm was said to be a place of hiding for wanted Nazis but as of yet no evidence could substantiate this claim. The Irish government never did issue him with a residency visa.

Skorzeny's name was at the top of the list of Nazi hunter Simon Weisenthal. Mossad agents (Israeli Intelligence) in early 1962 befriended Skorzeny as undercover German tourists. They claimed to have been robbed and required help. Over a few drinks and harmless flirtations, Skorzeny invited them to his villa in Madrid. Skorzeny made the couple, and pulled out his gun, "I know who you are and why you are here. You are Mossad and you've come to kill me!" at which the couple answered, "If we had come to kill you Skorzeny, you would have been dead months ago."

The couple were there to make Skorzeny a deal. He was worth more alive than dead. They needed his services and in exchange would pay a considerable sum. But Skorzeny wanted to be removed from Wiesenthal's list and they agreed. Little did he know the Mossad wouldn't keep their end of the deal.

At the end of the war, former SS commander Hermann Braun, who had been the commandant of the Auschwitz concentration camp from 1943 until 1945, lived in Southampton as a wood chipper and was also on Wiesenthal's list. During the Frankfurt Auschwitz trials, a warrant was placed for his arrest and his photograph was printed in newspapers. After seeing a wanted photograph in The Daily Telegraph, Amalie was on the next train. Amalie overheard that a co-worker had recognised his photograph and alerted local officials to his whereabouts. When Amalie confronted *"Fischer"* on an early October morning in 1960, he at first denied his true identity. His wife had accidentally revealed his identity, and within a few minutes of having her fingers pried off with a pair of pliers, she told Amalie of his whereabouts. She had theoretically dropped a bollock when she introduced herself as "Frau Braun" but then insisted her husband was called Fischer. Amalie crinkled her nose and looked towards the sky, 'I smell bullshit.' Amalie kicked open the door. Frau Braun squealed like a pig.

'Please, it is Mengele you are after,' he whimpered.

'Where is Mengele?'

'I don't know. Please,' he pleaded, 'OK, the last I heard, he sailed to Argentina but that was July, 1949.'

'That was easy wasn't it? Where is he headed?'

'Buenos Aires, I don't know anymore and you won't find him,' Braun smiled.

'Someone will. He'd be one lucky son of a bitch if I don't find him.'

'Where is my wife?' The realisation suddenly dawned on him that his wife was inside the house cooking dinner while he was in his shed chopping wood for the fire.

'I assume you are referring to the woman that greeted me at the door? She, who introduced herself as Frau Braun?'

'Oh dear lord...what have you done to her?'

'She's still alive, I will spare her life so she can live knowing how her husband was tortured and murdered.'

'I was just following orders! Please, I will scream!'

'Don't get me excited,' Amalie replied.

Braun had been one of the SS officers who helped unload the new arrivals at Auschwitz. Mengele would flick his riding crop left or right to indicate where that individual was to go; left to the gas chambers or right for hard labour. She remembered it like it was yesterday, Mengele with his evil grin. And, unlike many officers, he'd always arrive sober so he could savour every moment. Braun and other officers had been given strict instructions to find twins, giants, dwarfs or anyone in particular that had an unusual hereditary difference. Amalie heard an SS officer shout "Zwillinge!" *Twins!* in German and watched as parents were frantic over whether it was good or bad to be a twin. They saw barbed wire, the black smoke from the chimney, and often parents would announce they had twins believing it was a way out. Those that kept quiet and evaded discovery accompanied their parents to the gas chambers.

Since they were Mengele's children, they often were allowed to keep their hair. Amalie could spot a

Mengele twin solely because of their physical difference.

As a Kapo's first hand, Amalie was in close quarters of the twins. Every morning their lives began at 6.00 am. Like Amalie, they were required to attend roll call, eat a small breakfast, and await inspection by Mengele. His presence didn't bring fear; in fact, Amalie witnessed him offering chocolate. He would pat them on the head and even play with them. Eva Edelmann, a young twin, often called him "Uncle".

Amalie observed with fascination. *Why did they get special treatment?* The other prisoners were jealous and hurled verbal abuse. It wasn't fair, twins were spared punishment and were too young to sympathise with the labourers. It wasn't until the trucks arrived that Amalie realised why.

When Eva Edelmann returned, she was sad. The girl just stood there, like a statue. Sad sounds so insignificant to the reality of what had unfolded. Sad represented something that was able to be cast off. No, not sad, Eva was void. She had marks on her arm from where blood had been drawn, and she never did speak of what happened to her twin.

Mengele forced twins to undress and lie next to each other. He would examine their anatomies, searching for differences or similarities that distinguished the two, what was hereditary and what was different. Were the differences a result of environmental factors? Twins could be gone for hours.

Eva's fourth truck journey had been her last, and Amalie never saw her again.

CHAPTER 27

"If you can't beat them, bluff them"
N.R Kudelis

England in the 1950s was coming out of its post-war doom and gloom, and soon London became one of the most exciting cities in the world. Taking advantage of this was a man called John Aspinall, a man who always aspired to greater achievements. He had been born in India into a colonial middle-class family. In England, he tapped into an aristocratic weakness – gambling.

In the 1950s gambling was illegal, and Aspinall spotted an opportunity to hold illegal gambling parties at the homes of his wealthy friends in Belgravia. For years London's highest society gathered trustingly at John Aspinall's discreet tables. Those that attended were not only wealthy but respectable and included Lord Derby who, in 1958, lost over £20,000 at an illegal game of Chemin de fer.

It wasn't until the 1960s when gambling became legal that Lord William attended one of the games. William never played and neither wanted the media publicity were he to face an open court for "frequenting a common gaming house", but that didn't stop one of Aspinall's associates trying to unsuccessfully use him as his personal bank to socially advance himself.

When gambling became legalised, the Clermont Club at 44 Berkeley Square in Mayfair had been the first casino to be granted a licence. It opened its doors in 1962, and attracted celebrities and royals worldwide. It was described as more of a private London house than a casino. And according to David Wynne-Morgan who attended some of Aspinall's games, Aspinall "did it with style, he had wonderful taste. There was an infectious magnetism about the man that was really quite remarkable".

When word reached gangster Billy Hill, who was linked to smuggling and extreme violence, that Aspinall was in financial trouble, it was Hill's opportunity to infiltrate Britain's growing gambling culture. It was then he discussed his proposal for the Big Edge where John Aspinall snatched the idea out of his hands. The Big Edge scam ran for months turning into millions of pounds that the pair scammed and divided between themselves.

William remembered his first encounter with Billy Hill; he was charming, sure, and had a twinkle in his eyes, but he was as pale as a glass of milk. He was vigilant, with wide eyes and his hair was black and slicked back. His movements were slow as if he didn't have any bones, and he'd rub his hands together in that classic villain way. He didn't pretend to be anything other than what he was. He enjoyed making money and to him, robbing the rich was a game.

William had heard from DCI Owen that the home secretary had authorised the tapping of Hill's phone in late 1956, but William wasn't about to help the guy out. In fact, William didn't say much around Hill at all. He knew Hill wasn't someone to cross. He was especially sure after hearing Hill say, "I was always careful to draw my knife down on the face, never across or upwards. Always down. So if the knife slips you don't cut an artery. After all, chivving is chivving, but cutting an artery is usually murder. Only mugs do murder".

William would bet his bottom dollar that it was an associate of Hill that had informed Charrière of Amalie's extracurricular activities and who had placed the hit. Billy was known as the Boss of Britain's Underworld and working with Jack Comer, another notorious British gangster. They had made huge profits from brothels, and it was probably out of laziness that he didn't go to Paris to execute the narcissistic pervert himself – that was something Hill didn't want to be associated with. Hill liked to carve a "V" sign into his victim's foreheads and insisted that chivving was deployed only as a last resort.

New on the scene were brothers Reggie and Ronnie Kray; and as they came to prominence in London, Hill decided to leave crime. Hill would stand there in his suede shoes, his double-breasted suit, his trilby hat, and cigarette, and Reggie Kray would admire him as his role model. William even witnessed Reggie claiming that during his early 20s, the man he wanted to emulate was now former gang boss Billy Hill, "He had a good, quick thinking brain" Reggie would say.

The Krays sought publicity and in doing so allowed a journalist, John Pearson, into their lives. They loved having their photograph taken whilst rubbing shoulders with celebrities, and Ronnie even claimed whilst in court for his murder trial that he'd "be having tea with Judy Garland" if he hadn't been at court.

Amalie looked at the photograph of the Krays in The Telegraph and scrunched it up. As far as she was concerned, the higher the notoriety the more you were a target for the authorities. She'd rather stay in the shadows. She didn't care about her portfolio, showcasing her face so that she was feared and her demands more easily met. No, not Amalie, she'd look the bastards in the eyes; that's when they saw her face, that's when they knew whom to fear.

CHAPTER 28

I felt sorry for myself because I had no shoes –
until I met a man who had no feet.

Frau Braun was crouched in the corner of her home in Southampton when DCI Owen, Steve Harrison, and the rest of MI6 arrived. She had mentally shut down, and her forehead glistened with cold sweat as her wide eyes stared at the floor as if anticipating a final blow.

'Mrs Braun?' Harrison questioned with his notepad in his hand.

'Frau Braun,' corrected Owen. Harrison gave him a stern look.

Owen poured Frau Braun a drink and bent down to hand it to her. 'Shit, Harrison, call a doctor! Some of her fingers are missing.'

Frau Braun couldn't speak. She hung by a thread, barely audible as she sobbed. She mumbled and drew short gasps of breath, followed by shaking and bursts of hysterical sobbing, stopping only while trying to breathe again.

'Where is your husband Frau Braun?' Harrison's question raised a scream that could be described as nothing but primal.

As Owen left her with Harrison, he looked around the property in search of Frau Braun's husband, Hermann. He crouched towards the ground placing a hand on the dirt to take a closer look at spatters of blood that suggested he was near to a crime of some sort. There wasn't the odd drop that indicated a bleeding nose or a cut on a finger; pints were trailing like a crimson river. He took out his camera; a Beier Beirette. Crime scene photography wasn't Owen's favourite task, but it would be added to his portfolio of photographs he had taken; his portrait of time so to speak. He was always fascinated at one of the strange anomalies he harboured; how wherever he went he searched for details that were overlooked by the average person. He looked at things in a slightly abstract way, and if he was dining, his eyes might wander to a wine glass and he'd think, "That's a nice fingerprint". For John Owen, every case was being aware of what's going on in that scene and was there more than what met the eye?

Owen brought the camera close to his eye to take the shot. He wouldn't get a second chance to capture the images. He took satisfaction in knowing the effort he put in to capture the small details would be rewarded at the other end, however insignificant others deemed his efforts to be. As he manually focused the lens on the droplets of blood, Owen recognised the blood's freshness, and he withdrew his gun.

A neighbour had complained about a constant hum of machinery and dutifully called the local police. PC Pauls had been on duty at the time and attended the call. Shortly after arriving, MI6 had been informed. Pauls hadn't thought to turn the machinery off, but just pointed in the general direction of where Owen had to go.

As Owen followed the bloody trail he peered into the shed, suspicious of the stillness and calmness around the whirr. He staggered at the sight of Frau Braun's husband; what was left of him anyway. The machine shook side to side; Owen couldn't find a kill switch. He remembered when he was young his father had one similar and would laugh as Owen would look all around in search for it. His father just said, "Come on boy, choke it, starve it or stall it". That was it, simple and no safeguards.

Owen's stomach churned heavily. There was no body; there was just blood and lots of it. It was a real-life horror show. Never had Owen seen so much blood, it was one of the most harrowing things he had come across in his career. A coldness embalmed him as his hairs rose on the back of his neck and his mouth went dry. As the machine came to a stop, Owen noticed something odd. As he peered inside he saw a severed foot perched on top of a rock that was blocking the chute.

'Flipping heck, Owen,' said Harrison near the door.

'Stay there,' Owen replied. His fear was tangible and the menacing aura that pervaded the room held him in a tightening grip, but he steadied his breath to calm his panic. Part of him wanted to run, but he hadn't come this far to flee just yet.

Owen felt a sense of inquisitiveness. As he looked closer he could see a message written on the sole.

Have I put my foot in it this time Owen?

'She was here, wasn't she?' stated Harrison.
'Perhaps.'
'This bitch is a cold calculating narcissist with the

moral empathy of bacteria. Now she's playing with us.'

Detectives raided the area and had promising lines of inquiries, but Owen knew who had been here. Owen had taken a photograph of the message written on the foot and would add it to his wall in his bedroom.

Whilst Harrison filled in the other Detectives, Owen withdrew his sketch of the mystery woman and showed it to Frau Braun. 'Is this her?' Frau Braun's eyes widened and she screamed. He quickly shoved the drawing back into his pocket before Harrison came back.

It was concluded later in the investigation it was Hermann Braun's body that had been fed through the wood chipper. The blood spatter outside, according to the coroner, included ounces of human tissue and the crown of a tooth.

Owen went to the coroner's office, the Crowner, where the medical examiner would retain the foot for further investigation.

'No point in asking if there is any foul play.' Owen dryly stated as he walked in the door.

'DCI John Owen, it's a pleasure,' the coroner smiled. He was a soft-spoken man with a distinctive eloquent and formal tone. Owen had the utmost respect for Thomas Croker and found him consistently professional. He was a man in his sixties with short brown hair and grey eyes who favoured formal wear when he was not working in the field, and could often display an evil sense of humour. He drove a Morris Crowley, and it was always a topic of discussion during Owen's visits.

'Thomas.' Owen nodded, 'I thought this was a little outside your jurisdiction?'

'My patch is about 40 miles from one end to another, Owen.'

'Plenty of scope of people dying to keep you busy.'

'Oh indeed, the workload is always lightened up when we have Bennett around.'

'Bennett?'

'The ever-excellent Detective Chief Superintendent Bennett. He drops in for coffee and doughnuts early in the morning and tells me about the latest murders. He's great fun. Bennett reckons this area has a lot of domestic murder, and he jokingly always gives me advice, you know, that should I decide to kill my partner…not intentionally, of course, then the best thing I could do would be to ring and say I've done it, because as soon as you start prevaricating you've had it.'

'I'll keep that in mind. What do you make of this foot?'

'Domestic murder?' He laughed.

'Doubtful.'

'I was….never mind. Not a great deal at the moment I'm afraid,' he answered, frowning his brows that Owen hadn't seen the humour in his joke.

'You've got more chance than anyone understanding the language of the dead.'

'I gave my findings to Bennett earlier. It had crossed my mind whether it was connected to another case we're working on.'

'I've not been informed about this?'

'A couple of months ago on a cold morning, a father and son spotted a strange object floating at the shore's edge. Initially, they thought it was an animal, but as they ventured closer they saw it had a larger more familiar shape; it was a human torso. They immediately called the police, and that's when I was called. On initial inspection, the torso measured 20 inches. I could establish it was a white male and that it had been dismembered by a chainsaw due to cuts and partial ripping of the intestine where it had caught in the chain. It's currently an ongoing investigation as detectives continue their search for other body parts to help identify the victim.'

Owen left the Crowner after his dutiful goodbye. He knew the two cases weren't related, and he pondered whether Harrison also had come to the same conclusion so he wouldn't have to involve Owen on this case.

The foot had been severed and purposely left for Owen's eyes as a grisly show, almost in a theatrical way.

Her savage obsession of avenging her family's death had consumed her, and she didn't care in any conventional moral sense, nothing she did was evil because she didn't have any moral sense. Owen knew she had become hard-wired to do what she was doing through circumstances beyond her control, and he didn't have a name for what she was. Was she a monster? Like how we'd imply she was incomplete like someone born with missing limbs, so to speak? She was anything but, her murders were outlandish and flamboyant; these two cases were not connected.

CHAPTER 29

*"Can you remember who you were before the
world told you who you should be?"*
Charles Bukowski

The warm sun of the day's morning sky beat down onto Amalie's arms. She observed the chaos unfolding as the police car came screeching down the driveway; her knight on his white charger, his black tyres screeching as it came to a stop. She smiled as Owen exited the vehicle and walked towards the Braun residence. The cloudless day and bright blue sky were brilliant against the green shrubbery where she was hiding, it felt picture perfect. The screaming from Frau Braun made Amalie shake her head, and she focused as she watched Owen slip on some overshoes and then leave the house. The air was crisp, and she was careful not to let her warm breath give her location away, but she was fascinated and had Owen squarely in her sights. His sunglasses were dark, reflective, and seamless, and he was the epitome of authority. Perhaps it was the way he moved, the self-confidence? As he turned, she caught the fleeting look on his face. By now he had removed his glasses. She couldn't see his eyes, but his face was taut with concern. She watched with anticipation as he entered the shed, and she smiled.

Amalie could be both breathtakingly beautiful and anonymous at the same time. She was nothing before her uncle took her in and her training at the Brecon Beacons to become a purpose-built contract killer. Her instructions were simple – no questions asked, just dispatch individuals in various countries. She didn't care how many people were added to her list, it gave her a lifestyle, and one she had come to enjoy.

She was outwardly charming, educated and charismatic yet something dark lurked behind her eyes. You can't read her face or read her thoughts because something was missing. In Amalie's world, she was a master, but to The Brotherhood she was becoming a nuisance.

Owen lay on his bed and stared at the ceiling. He glanced over at the photographs on the wall.

'What am I missing?' he said to himself.

He looked back and forth at Helga Oppenheimer's crime scene, then Hermann Braun's. It was clear the killer was non-gender specific, but both victims suffered. Both were vengeful killings and both were war criminals. Owen knew too well what revenge was like; it haunted him every day gnawing at his soul like a rat on a piece of wood, unceasing and it only stopped by scratching the itch. His need for revenge festered, and he would bear that grudge until he died. He *couldn't* get his revenge, he never did find out what happened to his father. Owen knew whoever this killer was that her inner peace had been shattered, she had scores to settle and this wasn't the end of it. *What would I have done if I were in her situation?* He asked himself.

Owen had his suspicions of Harrison and the other agents, what were their motives? Why weren't they interested in *her* motives?

It wasn't likely a murdered gang member in France was a related crime, but that, too, was a showy display. Why else remove his penis? What male contract killer would have been able to get close enough to a high profile pervert in a brothel?

'She's just your average, garden variety nutter, Owen.'

'There's just one anomaly with all the victims.'

'They're crooks?'

'Besides that, they're all bad people.'

'How many more people, good or bad, have to die Owen?' Harrison snapped.

'You need to wake up, Owen. She is a remorseless assassin and she *will* kill you.'

'No, she won't.'

'She knows who you are. Do you really believe that?'

'Yes.'

'Tell us, John, why are you and this temptress so obsessed with one another?' another agent asked.

'I HAVE TO FIND HER. SHE WANTS TO BE CAUGHT. SHE WANTS ME TO CATCH HER.'

'So far we have nothing, Owen, for all this time she has eluded us. She's getting away with murder, and then she writes to you. Why?'

It was as if Amalie had fallen off the face of the earth, but the case remained very much open for MI6; at least until she was caught. Theorists and psychologists drafted a few papers stating it was safe to believe the eccentricity of her actions would eventually drive her insane. Some stated she was already dead.

The severed foot bore no forensic evidence. No other information or proof Amalie was at the scene unfolded, but DCI Owen felt sure it was her.

'Why you, Owen?' Harrison appeared infuriated and frustrated all at the same time.

'I don't know, you tell me. I don't pretend to know her any better than any of you.'

'Well, there is certainly something about *you* she likes.'

'Likes?'

'Ever thought that she might like you, Owen?'

'I think I amuse her.'

'Ever *felt* that she liked you?'

'I think she's a very bright young woman. I think she enjoys toying with her *interests*.'

'So far we know of three confirmed deaths at her hands, two of which were war criminals – they were of *interest* and look how that turned out.'

Harrison brought up the recent deaths to grasp Owen's attention and usually added that shock factor when he was trying to get to the point, 'Did you know, Owen, that apart from Frau Braun, there is another victim still alive?'

'The cockney?'

'Yes, he was treated at the Royal. He reckons he's got something that might help and wants to speak with you.'

'Why me?'

'Find out what you can, bring it back, and we'll use it. And Owen, be careful. This guy's not pretty.'

Harrison saw this as a perfect opportunity for Owen. Ever since Christie, Harrison had tried to get Owen on board, but as he climbed the ladder to stardom, it rubbed other agents up the wrong way. Owen was the perfect officer but no one wanted him as a partner. He didn't have a fragile ego, and life offered no shades of grey. It was black or it was white, it was that simple and Harrison respected that. He knew Owen wanted to catch this femme fatale, but the truth was far more complicated than that.

CHAPTER 30

"You have witchcraft on your lips".
William Shakespeare

DCI Owen knocked at the door of the house belonging to Percy Tunberry. The colossal structure hadn't been what Owen expected. As he drove up the driveway, the mansion loomed ahead. It was a house that just didn't know where to stop. No one had ever heard of it, no postman had ever delivered to it; no milkman had been brave enough to enter the ornate iron gates. It was a wonder if wildlife were brave enough to venture inside the grounds.

As the door opened, a butler guided DCI Owen inside. The ornate chandeliers, a long polished wooden table, and old oil paintings were what you would expect rich people to buy when they are paranoid about having too much money and start to shut themselves off from the rest of the world. It was indeed a beautiful prison.

'You must be DCI Owen? Mr Tunberry will be with you shortly.'

The dining room was a grand space, the huge wooden table took up most of the space that the romantic room offered, and you'd be foolish to place anything upon the table and ruin the perfectly varnished finish with your unworthy greasy fingers. Yet, like the rest of the house, the table's wood was probably fabricated from stolen railway sleepers, stripped, varnished and mounted – to hide their origins. There was definitely something sinister about this house.

'Edwin?' a quiet voice asked the butler as the man descended the staircase, 'Do I smell bacon?'

'No, Mr Tunberry, just someone left the pigpen open and one has arrived at your door.'

'Now, now, no need to be rude. Go on. Run along.' Mr Tunberry waved his hand to shoo the butler away.

'DCI Owen,' a voice quietly whispered.

'I am he.' Owen's voice didn't suit him.

'So, I hope I didn't frighten you?'

'Not at all, if you don't mind I'd like to get straight to the point!'

'Cup of tea?'

'No, thank you. Mr Tunberry. Had you ever seen this woman who did... this to you before?'

'No. Are ya' sure? I'm boiling the kettle.'

'Positive.' Owen stated, and he looked back down at his notes.

'I'll tell ya' anything, the crown prosecutor has offered me immunity if I help you out.'

'I see.' Owen nodded.

'Yeah, so, what do ya' wanna know?'

'Can you please remove that lolly, you're not a ten year old, and if you don't cooperate I'll throw your arse in jail where you'll be sucking on something else! Tell that to your crown prosecutor.'

'OK! Take a chill pill.' Mr Tunberry backed away with his hands up in surrender.

'How did you meet her?' Owen asked sternly.

'I didn't *meet* her. She was with some older fella, thought she's a darned Forty-Four!'

Owen struggled to understand Percy, but he knew a Forty-Four referred to a whore in cockney terms.

'And then.'

'We had a little fun. Watched for a reaction but didn't see much. Hoped they'd be afraid, offer some money, but they just ran. *Afraid* – of us? Almost seems laughable now.'

'Go on.'

'Then, nothing, we lost them.'

'What happened next?'Owen probed.

'I helped Don pack up, an' headed home. That was the last I saw him. Certainly didn't expect that forty-four to turn up a few hours later.'

'She followed you home?'

'Must 'av!' he shrugged.

'And then.'

'I invited her in of course; ah knew she couldn't resist a bit of this. I showed her my *room* and my special toys. If ya' know what 'am sayin',' Percy winked.

'I know what you're saying...' Owen grimaced.

'Well, curious little bint she was. She wanted to see more. I thought to myself, you're gonna get fucked well and truly tonight.'

'And...did you?'

'What?'

'Have intercourse?'

'Nah, she just sat there. More of a voyeur I think.'

'Go on.'

'Well, her eyes were the palest of blue; I could've spunked right at them.'

'Please stick to the story.'

'Well, her eyes were almost white and she sat there, in the corner on the accent chair up there. She was transfixed, her legs were crossed and her arms were stretched out cupping her knee - most peculiar. Then she suggested strapping a belt around my neck. I mean whoa! Where did this bitch come from?'

'Please continue.'

'So, she stands up and reaches for my belt that I'd tossed on the floor. She was very elegant about it all, like a pro, ya' know.'

'Did she tell you her name?'

'Errm...now that ya' mention it, yeah. Viola.'

'What did *Viola* do next?'

'Ah yeah, back to that. So I'm on my knees holding the belt with one hand and whacking myself off with the other. She just sat there; her foot extended pushing against my chest while her hand pulls at the belt. Usually, it gets some reaction, ya know. But, nothing. Then she reaches for a capsule. I thought *where did she get PCP from?'*

'PCP being the psychedelic drug? Didn't that raise any alarms?'

'Ay come on, I was pullin' ma plonker in front of a beautiful woman. But I'm reformed now. I have forgiven her.'

'Are you a frequent user of PCP?'

'Do ya' wanna know what happened or are you just here to know about my sexual deviancies?'

'What have you forgiven her for?'

'After she popped it into my mouth, she tugged a little tighter. I was on top of the world! Woohoo. Then this small blade appeared. By now the drug must 'av, I think the doctor called it "induced a psychotic state", I don't know. I can't remember that bit. Apparently, it's normal to feel less pain – that must be true. I didn't feel a thing!'

'What did she ask you to do?'

'I remember she looked me right in the eyes and suggested, I gouged out one of my eyes.'

'Your report says you are lucky to be alive. The drug offered you enough anaesthetic during your ordeal for you to survive.'

'So, err, anything else. Wanna closer look?'

'No, that won't be necessary.'

'Well if that is all, DCI Owen, I'm due a nap.'

'Of course...'

As Owen left the dining room, he was escorted towards the front door.

'One more thing, if I may Mr Tunberry. What was the last thing she said before she left?'

'"What's done cannot be undone". What's that all about?'

Owen spent the rest of the day climbing through old books that belonged to his mother. He'd heard *that* expression before. As the hours passed he selected his last book and read aloud, 'Act 3, scene 2 "Things without all remedy should be without regard: what's done is done", and "give me your hand. What's done cannot be undone".'

"What's done is done", did *she* use the expression and the use of the word "done" in the sense of "finished", or "settled", a usage which dates back to the first half of the 15th century?

Was *she* relating to Lady Macbeth in the sense that being a woman interferes with her plans? To

Macbeth, femininity meant compassion, was our killer compassionate? *I doubt it.*

Macbeth continually tried to wash the blood from her hands. Was this *her* symbol of guilt? In the play, Macbeth grows ill, but it's not an illness a doctor can treat; it's not physical sickness. Was our seductress actually not OK with her actions? There certainly are no take-backs when it comes to murder. "What is done *is* done".

And then he realised.

CHAPTER 31

"Only those who are prepared to go too far can
possibly know how far they can go."
Ernest Hemingway

Even while Amalie stood in front of Owen in his front
room he was mesmerised and could not capture who
she was as a person. He pondered how she came
about knowing where he lived.

'Don't run.' Amalie said, but Owen gasped and ran
as quickly as he could towards his gun. Amalie
seemed to be two steps ahead; she anticipated his
every move, and Owen felt possessed that someone
could captivate him as Amalie had. He felt himself
banging his head against a wall, his attraction
frustrated him. He reached for his gun.

'You don't want to do that,' she whispered.

'Why not...?' He reached as quickly as he could
for his gun and was met with a body slam from
Amalie.

'Damn it!' she snarled and her eyes locked on him,
'Can we just not think about work for a while?'

'Are you going to kill me?' he gasped.

She shook her head side to side. 'But that depends
on you.'

'Promise me?'

'You have my word.'

'I'm going to kill *you*,' he stated.

'If you were going to kill me, you would have
done it already. You like the chase. I can see it in

your eyes,' she smirked. 'Are you afraid?'

'No.'

'You should be.' Amalie smelled his cologne.

'I know something horrific happened to you and you're a very, very bright young woman.'

Amalie laughed, 'Why are you following me, why can't you leave me alone?'

'You know I can't do that.'

'You're out of your depth. You have no idea what you're getting yourself into. I heard you paid a visit to Percy. Ugly little fucker isn't he?'

'I didn't look.'

'Of course, you did. Everyone will now. Tell me, did he answer the door in that ghastly net he wore as a top?'

'Net?'

'Yes, he looked like he was trying to fit into a sprout bag! Has his DIY home surgery paid off? Has it improved his appearance? You don't have to answer that; he won't be getting his perv-pointer out any time soon after that experience. I can sincerely say he was definitely cheated by Mother Nature in that department.'

'Why did you do it?'

'So you want to know the *why* now do you?'

'I want to know everything about you.'

'You're going to get yourself killed.'

A knock sounded at the door. Amalie grabbed her coat.

'I'll be seeing you again,' she winked.

The knock came quietly at first. Then silence.

'Owen, are you in there?' The knock was louder and faster the second time around. He stood staring at

Amalie who stared at the door unmoving. 'You better get that,' she smiled.

'Let me in, Owen. I've got a lead,' the voice from the other side declared.

'This isn't over. You won't get away with what you're doing.'

'What you need to ask yourself Owen is; do you know the difference between obsession and desire? I'll be seeing *you* again.'

As the door opened, Amalie kissed Owen on the cheek. 'Thanks, John for a great evening. I'll be in touch,' she said in her best British accent. The elocution lessons paid off.

The man at the door was Harrison. His eyes widened. 'Sorry, did I interrupt something?'

'No, please come in.' As he closed the door, Amalie disappeared into the darkness.

'It has come to my attention, Owen, you know more about this woman than you're letting on.'

'Is that a fact?'

'Yes, and I've had no choice but to disclose your findings. These bastards want your head and I'm in two minds to feed it to them.'

'Do you want her alive?'

'I need to know that I can trust you.'

'You don't?'

'Don't make me regret my decision to promote you.'

'I'll get you your girl, but you need to let me do my job.'

'If you take your ego out of the equation I'd have more faith.'

'Will that be all?'

Steve Harrison's ability to run MI6 had been questioned in the past several times. More recently he had been the subject of review when one of his agents had shot the Congo's first democratically elected Prime Minister, Patrice Lumumba, in '61.

Beforehand, the Foreign Secretary had ordered Harrison to remove an agent from the field and stop any investigations in the terrorist organisation.

'I'll expect you tomorrow morning, at 9:00 sharp. You're going undercover.'

CHAPTER 32

"Are you going to bark all day, little doggy, or are you going to bite." Mr Blond, Reservoir dogs.

Charlie Evans, a member of The Brotherhood, was a variety of his own. He'd kidnap to order. For a set fee, he'd swipe anyone, any status, age, or gender. Then he would drop them off at the required location and time with no questions asked. The business was great; so many people were wanting to do bad things without getting caught. For Charlie, it made it simpler and his clients always paid in advance. He had a reputation to uphold, and that was as one of London's most sadistic gangsters. You'd never see him in the same room as the Kray twins, they detested each other, and Charlie was mainly based in south London anyway until he was hired elsewhere. Charlie Evans was known to have cut toes off with bolt cutters, nail his victims to the floor or even electrocute them until they were unconscious and pull their teeth out with pliers.

'I want him brought to me alive, untouched,' the client asked.

Up to now, Evans had successfully managed to remain fairly undetected by the police. Charlie would be your typical British Goodfella; he dressed elegantly, posed in sophisticated restaurants, and exuded a glamour that attracted the likes of blond bombshell Diana Dors to flirt around him. At just thirty years old he had become a wealthy man, now owning seven scrap yards. His victims were tortured at one of his scrap yards, and if they survived, were told to clean up their own blood. But this job was different. He couldn't torture this one. It would be his head if he did. He stared at his target for a while, visualising scenarios of what he could do, but instead just walked straight up to them. His target looked at him in the eyes, and with a gun pointed at their chest, they knew that backing out wasn't an option.

'Boss wants to see you.'

His victim nodded and followed him towards the car. Charlie Evans had never heard of Lord William, it was the first time he had ever laid eyes on him. William promised him money, but Evans wasn't interested.

He took his brown envelope with his payment and walked out the door, no questions asked, just as his client had liked it.

William waited in the abandoned warehouse, tied to a chair, untouched, just as Charlie had promised. William bore no facial expression.

'Is this necessary?' he asked as the shadowy figure strolled towards him. It was Tommy Hunt, also known as, "The Butcher".

Last week Hunt had sunk a knife into someone's eye for questioning his motives, William gulped. Hunt had no sense of right or wrong, he had no moral compass.

'Please sit down,' Hunt gestured, smirking, as William was tied to a chair. 'Didn't you get the memo? Control your animal or I will.'

'Are you taking the piss?'

'You looked shocked,' Hunt replied.

'You're making a mistake.'

'You and your little sweetkin have caused me and my fellow friends considerable consternation.'

'I have no idea what you're talking about.'

'The amount of trouble she has caused. I mean, Percy, poor Percy. That fucker would have been better off dead if I'm honest with what she did to his face. Don't even get me started on this little revenge saga of hers.'

'He had it coming and so did those bastards.'

'I think it will be in your best interest if we finish this here and now. Do you understand?'

'It doesn't matter what I say or do, the fact is, she *will* find you before you find her.'

'Oh, I'm banking on it.'

Tommy was an A-class creep. He wasn't a big man, but he'd beat anyone smaller than himself to a pulp, and Amalie was his next target.

Underground gangland boss Billy Hill wasn't known for his patience. He committed his first stabbing at fourteen but he was never tried for murder. He stabbed, battered, or bullied his way to the top of London's mob. Hill quickly realised that crime paid, his scam with Aspinall became one of the most outrageous cons of the era and remained undetected for two years. It was ended by John Aspinall only when his partner, John Burke, decided to retire. Burke cut links with Hill stating, "It's becoming too difficult to conceal". Amazingly and uncharacteristically Hill agreed.

Hunt idolised Billy Hill, many did, and he felt on top of the world. 'Women, everywhere I tell you.' He'd laugh with fellow diners as the waiters would fill their glasses. He'd joke and gamble wildly and brag about the wealth and power he thought he deserved. But, he had a problem that gnawed at him. One only he could deal with, and that was Amalie. He hoped kidnapping William would bring her out of the woodwork, but she was far too clever for that. He had to think of something else.

'You see, William, you're a bright man, and one day it might be you standing here in front of some wayward ponce telling them about the way it is. You start at the bottom, you're someone's dog. After a few kicks, you start to bite back. Get kicked less 'til one day you're in Elysium and you forget what a foot even looked like.'

Tommy untied William and gestured he follow him outside where a car was waiting. He pushed William's head into the back of the car.

'This ends now. Remember, William, "power, money, and then respect".'

CHAPTER 33

"Yesterday you said hi to me and I died."

Harrison's lead was nothing more than what Owen already knew.

'Do you have any idea where she might be going?'

'No, I've none at all.'

'No hunches?'

'Nope.'

In reality, his brief encounter with *her* only made him more curious. He thought about her every day; who she was with, what she was doing, what she was wearing, what she ate, and when he would see her again.

Steve Harrison liked Owen, but the other agents didn't, especially Agent Morley. They resented the DCI's promotion that in their opinion he didn't deserve, and to justify their resentment they would say he was a cock-sucker. The sooner he was out of MI6 the better. DCI John Owen definitely had to go. Left to his own devices, his instinct, charisma and style, being virtually friendless and intensely solitary, DCI John Owen *would* find Amalie Keller.

When Owen wasn't reporting secret intelligence back to MI6, he carried on life as usual working alongside PC Reese or "*PC Plonker*" as William had once called him. It had become a tremendous added stress and a psychological strain for Owen to live the secret life. No one knew about his connections to MI6, and his security briefings had become second nature. Had he been chosen for his ability to thwart assassinations or was it because he didn't have a nearest and dearest? Regardless of The Secret Intelligence Service's motive, Owen enjoyed it. He liked the thrill the job offered; of course, working for the Secret Service didn't come free of danger.

Throughout the weekend, Owen had a few leads to chase. He swivelled in his office chair at home twiddling a pencil between his fingers when a car caught his attention.

Agent Morley's car came to a screeching halt. As a cop car, the instantly recognisable Ford Cortina was as subtle as a freshly squeezed spot, and in this case, just as welcomed. Morley in his white charger checked his hair in the mirror and exited his vehicle.

John could see him through the window as Morley headed for his front door. When the doorbell rang, he thought twice about answering it. He didn't need any more chauvinistic comments in the privacy of his own home.

Owen answered the door. He was rarely seen dishevelled and took pride in his appearance. His trousers were a dark classic cut, no pleats and no turn-ups. They were simple yet elegant, and his shirt was clean, white, and crisp. Only his Heuer watch offered any insight into anything personal about John Owen – *he had good taste.*

'Hi, Owen.'

'Morley, come in.'

'I'd like that very much but I can't stay long. Harrison asked me to drop this off.'

After Morley had finished blowing smoke up Harrison's arse and running errands like a good little puppy dog, Owen opened the letter; it read:

Dear John,
I have been following with intense earnestness
your success, and I'm almost positively sure that your
father as well is looking down with pride that his little
boy has such a promising future.

Before Owen continued, he nodded to Morley to leave. Owen read the letter hearing the words out loud as if she were speaking to him. And without finishing, he knew at once who had written to him. The envelope showed no signs of tamper, *had this already been read by MI6?* He closed the door, sat at his desk, and continued to read the letter whilst pushing back on his chair. He exhaled slowly and inhaled the scent of the letter. *Had she been bold enough to have delivered this herself and why to MI6?* From the handwriting and scent, Owen deduced the writer was female and it was our girl.

Your father, John, was a police officer and your
mother, a librarian. Was this life you lead your
choice or theirs? Is living a life of solitude your
choice or theirs? Would your dead father want you to
live a life of fear? Death is a fearful thing. You see
John; we are alike more than you think. "If you prick
us do we not bleed? If you tickle us do we not laugh?
If you poison us do we not die? And if you wrong us
shall we not revenge?"
I think about you often, funny isn't it? A few brief
meetings and yet the memory clings to you, they cling
like a decadent hope that should we ever speak or

meet again that feeling would remain. Have your colleagues teased you about the way you have obsessed over me since our first encounter? Maybe they make snide remarks; out of jealously, I'm sure.

Have you found someone you can relate to John, someone you can confess to? How about someone you can sexually confide in, have you found that person that is comparable in both intelligence and physicality? Balance is always good to have – wouldn't you agree?

Don't you, too, feel that vengeance is in your heart? Death is in your hand, blood and revenge are hammering in your head?

Please let me know.

Amalie Keller

Owen knew he had to find Amalie before someone else did, but he was crippled by a sense of self-consciousness and guilt. To him, Amalie saw the law as something to play and manipulate. She had no regard for right or wrong, and she showed no sign of stopping. *Was Amalie's obsession over Owen because he's this handsome Lothario? Owen didn't know.* Harrison was sharp and witty; his recruitment of Owen for the off-the-books assignment to track down Amalie had Owen's hair raised from the start. His erratic behaviour didn't correlate to understanding who this assassin worked for – he just seemed eager to *eliminate* her.

Owen had thought about Harrison's reaction to the letter – *he'd be thrilled* at the new piece of evidence. He would break the news with tact and discretion, keeping the contents of the letter from the other agents. Although he knew her place of residence, he was sure the other agents didn't.

CHAPTER 34

"These violent delights have violent ends".
William Shakespeare

Mrs Campbell shook like a leaf. She strained to speak, but her body quivered with a raw sob. Fright and anxiety consumed her, Amalie was losing patience.

'Where is Uncle?' Amalie's blood pressure began to rise, but she would never let Mrs Campbell see emotion – she had the uttermost respect for the woman.

Mrs Campbell described in detail the day William went missing. What he was doing, what car turned up and what the stranger looked like.

'Oh, Amalie, you must find him!'

'I will, Mrs Campbell! Do you know who took him?'

'No, I've never seen him before. But he was wearing a black suit and he stubbed his cigarette out on the flower bed and raised his head to look at the sky before he took William.'

'Did you see his car?'

'It was black, with black windows.'

She couldn't concentrate on anything else. In the silent panic, Amalie's wild eyes dilated. When Mrs Campbell stopped talking, Amalie knew there was a problem. Unbeknownst to Amalie, Mrs Campbell had already informed DCI Owen of William's disappearance.

The Star Tavern was a pub in the posh Belgravia neighbourhood. A 19th-century building built for servants of the wealthy. A hard gambler and larger than life Irishman called Paddy Kennedy took it over. It was common knowledge that he'd offer his customers what was called "the special treatment" where he'd swear and offer nonstop insults, and yet his clientele loved it. During the 50s and 60s, it won infamy for being London's local hangout for London's master criminals who drank alongside stars of the era such as Princess Margaret and British film and stage actor Peter O'Toole.

The toffs found it entertaining and dangerous all at the same time, hanging around with known criminals and being sworn at by the landlord regardless of who they were. The audacity of Paddy shocked his clients. He had no regard for his client's status or wealth – he treated everyone the same.

It hadn't been long since Belfast boy Peter Scott had robbed Sophia Loren, giving her what he described "what she deserved", and he was still the talk of the tavern. Other customers joked that Scott would call himself a modern-day Robin Hood and would describe how he eluded capture by donning a new suit and creep into the homes of some of London's richest. Even if he were interrupted he'd shout, "It's only me!" It meant he got away with his crimes. One of his victims was gambling club owner John Aspinall, of whom he recalled, "robbing that bastard Aspinall was one of my favourites". He'd joke at the bar "I hear poor Sophia has been robbed" whilst pulling out a wad of cash. If Amalie were to find out what had happened to William, she'd need to blend in and keep her ear to the ground.

Word went around among the wealthy where the fun was to be held and whose home was the chosen location for that particular game. Tonight was at the Kensington home of Mr and Mrs Clayton. It was an open house, unlike one of Aspinall's games where you'd need an embossed invitation as the acme of social acceptability.

The atmosphere was luxurious and amusing, there was laughter, drinking, and joking. But at the same time, it was big money. Amalie had her uncle's cheque book at the ready.

Amalie was among London's crème de la crème, and her facade of a Parisian actress fitted in perfectly. Although one of the main topics was the Clermont Club and its members, the subject moved to Ian Fleming.

'Did you hear Ian Fleming is playing over at the Clermont tomorrow evening?' one of the women at the table whispered to a fellow player.

'Ian Fleming, isn't he that author of those spy novels?'

'Yes, I'm hoping if I get an invitation he'll sign my copy of Casino Royale.'

'Doubtful.' Amalie mumbled.

'I'm sorry. Who are you?'

'Ginette Signoret,' Amalie answered. She charmed the two women at the table, convincing them she had catapulted to stardom acting alongside Brigitte Bardot. Famous in French cinema, her facade, Miss Signoret, was an entrancing, luscious lipped French leading lady, and she turned heads among the male compatriots.

Amalie loved pretending she was someone else, and she had become a pro delivering a flawless performance to her audiences. She would recall the deep recesses of her memory to capture her reality, portray that emotion, and twist it into anger, hope, persuasion and happiness. She loved it. For who could step into the role of a fictional character or even someone based on truth, and give it life? Amalie could. She had spent years trying to be someone else.

The woman next to her looked up at Amalie through her thick mascara, and her long gloved fingers pulled a cigarette from her pursed red painted lips. 'Darling,' she hollered at her husband, 'come here, this is Ginette Signoret, *and she's* an actress.'

Her husband approached Amalie with a grim smile, 'Madam, it is a pleasure. What brings you to London?'

'Marriage,' Amalie answered.

'Um... Ginette,' the woman placed her hand on Amalie's arm, 'please tell us what you're working on at the moment.'

'Les Bonnes.'

'What does that mean?'

'The Maids; it's a play, first performed at the Théâtre de l'Athénée in Paris. There will be a TV dramatisation right here in England.'

The couple looked intrigued. 'Did you ever hear of the infamous French Papin sisters, Lea and Christine Papin?'

'I can't say we have.'

'You must watch it, it's a recreation based on the two dutiful, quiet live-in housemaids to the Lancelin family.'

'It doesn't ring any bells.'

'Oh, you must see it. I play the character based on Christine – the middle sister. However, I won't be bludgeoning and stabbing someone to the point they become unrecognisable.'

'Excuse me?'

'Well, the *real* story is that Madame Lancelin's eyes had been gouged out and were found in the folds of her scarf that was still around her neck, while one of her daughter's eyes was found under her body and another on the stairs.'

'It sounds absolutely fascinating.'

CHAPTER 35

Revenge is best served cold.

The 1960s were considered the Diamond Decade. It was the second decade of the Queen's reign. The rise of the Beatles and The Rolling Stones happened in a period of significant social change. The "Swinging Sixties" saw growth in fashion, popular music, and cinema. It was also a time of technological progress. Together Britain and France developed the world's only supersonic airliner – Concorde, but it was also some time in 1960 that the amphetamine craze erupted in London's West End.

The Mod subculture emerged during the 60s, too, characterised by terms like cosmopolitan, cool, and even groovy. It was established in post World War II London by the youth of working-class families that were trying to adopt a more exciting and fashionable lifestyle. They wanted to give the impression of sophistication by wearing expensive clothing. They also enjoyed a very robust social life.

Amalie had successfully intrigued her companions from the evening before, and they had invited her to join them for a private evening at their home in Mayfair.

Tommy Hunt and his wife had no inclination that they had just let a Trojan horse into their home.

Mrs Hunt was in awe of Amalie, and she was to cause her own demise by being so vain.

As Mrs Hunt babbled about her wealth, Amalie

grew tired. Tommy Hunt was in the bathroom, hunched over the toilet. Amalie had spiked his drink.

'Are you admiring my diamond ring?' Mrs Hunt asked. Amalie had had enough, but she humoured Mrs Hunt. 'My husband bought it for my birthday.'

'That's nice,' Amalie smiled.

'And he bought me these for our anniversary,' she pointed to her ears.

'That's nice,' again Amalie replied.

'What did your fiancé spoil you with?'

'Elocution lessons.'

'Elocution? My dear, albeit with a French accent, your spoken English is perfect. For what reason has he given you elocution lessons?'

'I used to say *fuck you*, now I say *that's nice*.' Amalie grabbed her fork and rammed it into Mrs Hunt's eye socket.

Mrs Hunt was a habitual user of the new craze, using amphetamines in everyday use as a pick-me-up for the tired housewife. She never questioned her source, but it was a known fact that robberies of chemists and pharmaceutical companies were on the increase to satisfy the growing black market demand, and The Krays helped ship the amphetamines into the West End of London from their criminal mafia-style operation in the East End. Amalie hadn't been too concerned about the Kray twins' antics – they were gangsters in it for glamour and reputation; collecting protection money and comparing themselves to the likes of Al Capone. Amalie didn't need to pursue the Krays – they were already being watched by the authorities.

CHAPTER 36

*"Any woman can fool a man if she wants to and if
he's in love with her" Agatha Christie*

But the Krays were untouchable. The key member in
the scandal that enabled the Krays to run amok was
Lord Robert Boothby; a reckless gambler, bisexual
and drunkard. In 1964 he was one of England's most
famous politicians. He was made a peer in 1958 by
the Conservative Prime Minister Harold MacMillan, a
compassionate act as Boothby had been having an
affair with the PM's wife since the 30s. Many people
thought Boothby was destined for prime minister, but
one of his flaws was his desire to exaggerate. He
became a habitual member of casinos and constantly
ran short of funds. Consequently, his financial woes
would be a political disaster. He had been
Parliamentary Private Secretary to Winston Churchill
from 1926 until 1929 and was later appointed to his
wartime government as the Minister of Food from
1940 until 1941, but forced to resign for not declaring
an interest when asking a parliamentary question.
Boothby never forgave Churchill for that. Following
his resignation, when he made the speech in the house
of commons, he said, *"I admitted no guilt at any time,
except the guilt of being a gambler which I am by
nature and I've stuck to that ever since and of course,
that's what saved me because I couldn't have
survived if I had been guilty of anything beyond
that".*

His friends in high places kept any disparaging rumours away from front pages of Fleet Street, however his reasonably discreet activities were unravelled in the July of '64 as a Sunday newspaper ran an article reporting Scotland Yard was investigating the homosexual relationship between a well-known figurehead and a major figure in London's criminal underworld. It read:

"PEER AND GANGSTER: YARD INQUIRY"
Exclusive Society Mingling with Thugs in
London's Underworld.

It came at a time when Westminster was still flabbergasted at the Profumo affair. However, with the help of some influential friends, Boothby denied the rumour and the newspaper was forced to withdraw. He collected a large sum of money, around £40,000, after the newspaper outed his links with the Krays. Thereafter the media was scared off pursuing the story in case of another libel suit, but the matter eventually was reported in the German magazine *Stern*.

The Krays knew about Boothby's double life and came to meet him through another rogue politician who revelled in the companionship of criminals. He had taken Boothby to the gambling club run by the Krays in Knightsbridge which resulted in a friendship between politician and gangster. Bringing violent criminals into the social circles of lords and civil servants enabled the Kray brothers to enjoy a sense of power, ensuring that all of Boothby's perversions were satisfied.

Boothby was a conceited character, and as a well-known public figurehead, his movements were closely watched. The police were all too aware of his close relationship with the Krays as they tracked their involvement in extortion, fraud, protection rackets, and their large scale pimping organisation operated from a house in Suffolk owned by Ronnie Kray.

Boothby later admitted to having met the Kray twins for a few business meetings, but stated to the Home Secretary that he had not known the Krays were criminals, and later had refused the business plan that had been proposed. The Krays sought fame, and pursued being photographed with Boothby – after all, he was a political personality. They weren't at this particular point in time very well-known, but that was soon to change.

The Mirror dubbed the Krays as "dodgy trouble" after £40,000, and subsequently referred to them as "well-known sporting brothers". However, Detective Chief Inspector Leonard Read, also known as "Nipper", was keeping the Krays under close scrutiny. Nipper served as a petty officer in the Royal Navy during the Second World War and joined the Metropolitan Police Service in 1947. The police investigation received no support from Scotland Yard. Any journalists wanting to investigate Boothby further were subjected to legal threats, break-ins, and worse, and Scotland Yard had their eyes at Harrison's allegations of torture.

CHAPTER 37

The scars of our past remind us that it was real.

1969. The Beatles had their last public performance. France conducted its first test flight for Concorde. The iconic Pontiac Firebird Trans Am was introduced to petrol heads that were after that American muscle, and Charles Manson's cult murdered five people.

'What's your hunch, Owen?'

'I think she wants out. She wants out of this hold that *this* Brotherhood has over her.'

'I've told you before, The Brotherhood is not our concern, just find *her*,' Harrison snapped. 'This is Poppy Wright. If you want to find anything, anyone, anywhere, this is your girl.'

'Right,' Owen nodded.

'How may I be of assistance?' Poppy smiled.

Poppy's doe eyes looked at John, her thoughts barely forming to coherent sentences as she fantasised of what could be if only she were brave enough to say. She daydreamed over his facial features as he spoke and laughed oddly and out of place at his quirky mannerisms. Poppy had seen Owen before and had prayed that one day he would notice her. She hung onto his every word and laughed at his jokes, and when he spoke to her she sputtered something incoherent in response. As he sat next to her, she gulped and started to perspire.

'I'm looking for a young woman by the name of Keller.'

'Keller? What kind of parent calls their child Keller? *Kelllllerrrr, here Kelllerrr*?'

'Surname.'

'Oh, I see, rightio then.'

'Mid to late thirties, slim build, dark hair.'

'I'll see what I can find.'

Miss Wright informed Owen that she had tracked an A. Keller to an orphanage in East Germany, and that a horrific event occurred the day she left.

'That's got to be our girl.'

But nothing was recorded of her whereabouts thereafter.

'You could try asking Hilary Goldberg, she now resides in Milton Keynes. She might know something. Goldberg arrived the same day as Keller at the orphanage.'

Hilary Goldberg was born in Będzin, a city in Zagłębie Dąbrowskie, southern Poland. Before the invasion, Będzin had a vibrant Jewish community and the town's census showed in the early 20s that the Jewish population was around 17,500. By 1938, that number had increased to 22,500.

With just a photo to go on, DCI Owen arrived at the address.

Hilary's house was from the mid 20s, and Owen imagined it to have a secret cellar, like houses from prohibition times. The house, with its thatched roof and mullioned windows, looked like it belonged in a storybook. It was the kind of home that made Owen jealous.

He spotted her sitting on her porch in a large

wicker chair with her feet tucked underneath. She was knitting a jumper and mumbling an inaudible tune. Her raven black hair was braided to keep the strands off her face, and he reluctantly exited his car knowing he would ruin her day. As he walked up the path, she stopped rocking in her chair. Her eyes as blue as the sea looked upon him like dazzling gems and her lips were as red as cherries. Despite the appearance, Owen gripped his gun in its holster, and he offered her a slightly wry smile.

'May I help you?' she asked.

'Hello, my name is Detective Chief Inspector John Owen. I'd like to speak to you about an Amalie Keller?' he spoke softly.

The woman gulped and looked into her lap, 'Keller, now that's a name I haven't heard for a while.'

'If it wouldn't be too much trouble...'

'You had better come in.' Hilary stood up and placed her knitting to one side and gestured that Owen follow.

'Can I offer you some tea?'

'That would be wonderful. You have a beautiful home.' Owen stepped carefully into Hilary's home and looked around in awe. It had a hint of Lavender, and he could see a freshly picked bunch in old jars on her window sill.

'I always did like the simpler things in life,' she smiled as she watched Owen admire the purple bloom.

'A home is just space unless you bring your own personality into it.'

'Here's your tea, I couldn't agree more. Please,'

she waved towards her conservatory. 'I wouldn't want my husband to hear about this....he...doesn't need to know.' She looked at her husband tending to the flowers in the garden.

'I understand,' he smiled.

'Do you? You don't appear to be a survivor.'

'No, a victim I'm not,' he looked to one side.

'Correction, I did not say I was a victim.' She sipped on her china cup.

'You don't see yourself as a victim?' he queried.

'To call me a victim means they won, they didn't win. They didn't take what's inside here,' Hilary put her hand over her heart.

'I apologise. This by the way is the best tea I have ever tasted.'

'My husband comes from a long line of tea planters in Ceylon. I'd expect nothing less than perfection,' she smiled, 'and no, I should apologise. You came here to discuss Keller.'

'Yes...how do you know her?'

'How long have you got?'

'I'm not in any hurry if another brew is in the cards?'

'Certainly.'

Hilary stood up and made another cup of tea while Owen took out his notepad and tape recorder and started jotting down notes. As she placed a freshly made cup beside him, she looked him in the eye. 'I'll start from the beginning,' she pointed to his notepad, 'so that you get all the facts.'

'If you could start the interview by confirming your identity that would be grand; then you can start, is that OK?' she nodded in acceptance

'My name is Hilary Goldberg; I was born in a small town by the name of Będzin, also known in German as *Bendsburg,* in southern Poland in the year 1926. I am the daughter of a tailor and the third eldest of five children. We lived in an apartment at number 55 Modrzejowska Street across from where my father had his shop. I remember when I was thirteen years old, my friends told me about this invasion and I ran with them to all the commotion. No more than six hours after the invasion had our town been occupied by the Germans. We watched as the guns and Howitzers; that's a short gun for firing shells with the small calibre, we watched as they went off to, *well,* war. But, it was too late, we could hear the howl and the rolling of artillery, the war was coming to us. By the weekend, our small town had filled with thousands of other refugees from central Poland that were fleeing the fighting. I distinctly remember I didn't go to the school that following Monday, for me it was a day off and news had hit the town that the British and French were coming to our rescue. We all gathered to greet them but instead it was the *Wehrmacht;* armed forces of the Third Reich. We went home in confusion and didn't dare leave the house again. We huddled together listening to the shootings outside and my mother and father would cover our ears so we couldn't hear the screaming as perhaps around five hundred local people, people we knew, were murdered in the streets. But we were found, and I was taken to a Ghetto in Będzin *Ghetto von Bendsburg* on the same street we lived; Modrzejowska Street in 1942; I was just sixteen years old. I was sent to work in a textile factory producing uniforms for the German army. The owner was a man called Alfred Rossner; he took care of us, aided our family, and protected us from deportation. During the liquidation of the Ghetto, he concealed many of us under his management, but by 1943, the SS came, and no more than a month later he was executed by hanging. You see, anyone helping a Jew was punishable by death so for the SS, Rossner was certain death, especially due to his activities on behalf of the Jews. He was just thirty-seven when he died in January 1944. I remember Rossner walked with a pronounced limp along the rows of the machines and addressed us in Yiddish asking us about our families, we all adored him. He wanted to serve his country but he couldn't do it with a weapon in his hand so he'd bribe the SS by dressing them in uniforms and clothing made by the best tailors. It obviously worked as we were becoming busier. He asked the SS if they were happy with the production and asked them if we could receive more bread. They compromised that we would indeed receive extra bread provided we would have a 10% production increase. I believe it was Rossner's protection that helped me to survive until Będzin was liquidated.

'Conditions weren't improving and food was limited. My father and older brother were deported somewhere, I still don't know where. My mother, and my three sisters and I were sent for, *resettlement* I think they called it? We were loaded into a commuter train, we didn't at this point know of our destination but it *was* Auschwitz. While we waited to board, a man went up to an armed officer who was guarding us and asked who we were. When he answered "these are the enemies of our Führer" the man walked towards us and spat on us. I started to feel sorry for myself but Mother told me if I started that, I was soon to be a goner.

'We were among about 30,000 Jews that went to Auschwitz. Upon arrival, my mother and two sisters were pulled to one side and I, with my older sister by one year, Greta, went to the other side. I don't know why. But, she survived for four days before she too was marched to the gas chamber...' Hilary took a moment of silence.

'How did you survive?' Owen asked gently.

'Well, while the German Shepherds barked and kept us huddled before we were separated; a Kapo took our few belongings we'd been allowed to bring with us. She said, "I hope you understand you are going straight to your death?" I didn't believe it. My mother pushed me away and said that if I survived then part of her would as well. I never saw her again. After our heads and private areas had been shaved, they sent hundreds of us at a time into a chamber where we stood freezing and frightened. We weren't daft, we saw the smoke from the chimneys when we arrived and the air smelled; it smelled like burning flesh. Other prisoners whispered to us that the chambers were gas chambers. Everyone was crying, shivering and crying more. Was it water or was it gas? I felt at this point that absolutely nothing else in the world would cause so much misery than the uncertainty of our fate. It was water.

'After we dressed, we went to our accommodation that was actually designed for horses. The interior had been partitioned into stalls and each stall contained a three-tier bunk. The barrack had been built to house ideally 52 horses but there must have been some several hundred of us living there. That's when you started to feel dehumanised; when other prisoners suffered from diarrhoea, rats and a shortage of water and leaky roofs made even the difficult conditions even worse. By now the smell of excrement was a daily smell, but I could never get used to the cold. I remember one day I saw a patch of tomatoes and I was so hungry, I took one. The guards beat me so severely I ended up in hospital – black and blue I was. I still have the scars, look.

'So I asked a Kapo, as I was a skilled garment worker, if I could be of use. I knew if I was to dig trenches I wouldn't last long in the cold and I couldn't sing to entertain the soldiers, so I offered my services as a seamstress. I was tattooed here,' she rolled up her sleeve showing Owen her five-digit number imprinted on her forearm.

'Did it hurt?' Owen asked. Hilary roared with laughter.

'This? This was the least of my worries. I didn't know this at the time but the Nazis had this practice of *Vernichtung durch Arbeit...*'

'I'm sorry my German's a little rusty.'

'The destruction or extermination through labour, but working at the tailoring studio for me was salvation. Hedwig Hoess who was the wife of the camp's most feared commander Rudolf – *that bastard,* the shop was a haven from the horror and stench. Our instructions; to create an elegant evening gown. Of course that's what I had been doing before. I was in my element.'

'Didn't it bother you that you were creating such glorious garments and yet you were dressed in rags?' Owen scrunched his brow.

'No, not at all. If we could impress the sausage eating bastards we were awarded an additional piece of bread or we were allowed to wash or even sleep in a clean bed. We all had to, how do you say it in English? *Suck up?* We, as a family, never had much but we had each other; I grew up watching my father make the most beautiful clothing for other people and it made us happy because that's what gave us food. So, like with Rossner, if we wanted food, we would sew. At Auschwitz it was even more black or white; we had to sew to save our lives.

'On one occasion a female SS arrived for a fitting. With her was a small girl. I was required to alter clothing the girl had brought from the stockpile as well as that taken from other Jews who had arrived at the camp. The girl's beautiful blue eyes looked into mine and there I learned her name was Amalie. Amalie came almost every day, she couldn't have been more than ten years old, maybe a little older; it's hard to tell when they're that young and especially so thin, her breasts hadn't developed yet so she was definitely pre-teen.'

'Amalie was at the camp?'

'Well, of course. I thought you knew that?'

'No. No, I didn't. Please continue.'

'Amalie was or is Hungarian. You see, at the time of WW2 Hungary were allied with the Nazis so it became very difficult for Jewish families to live. Almost as if overnight, the law no longer protected them. I saw so many Hungarians at Auschwitz, all donning the yellow star. In just six weeks half a million Hungarian Jews were rounded up into 147 cattle carts and brought to Auschwitz – it still is so incomprehensible.

'Not a day passes where I don't think of my parents and siblings and all the other people that tragically lost their lives, and I feel lucky that I am here today to share my story. I'm forever grateful that I have a wonderful husband. We've both managed to hang in there; I never felt the need to see a psychologist and I don't think I ever will. To be honest, something like that you have to separate yourself as if it's not really happening, you're just role-playing because otherwise, if you allow it to penetrate, it will swallow you whole, and to this day I believe those that never managed to separate themselves died.'

'I find it absolutely incredible a young woman in that situation could find the strength, let alone a child.' John couldn't believe what he was hearing and shook his head in shame.

'Sorry, I got sidetracked. I was just thankful that I didn't have to stand in line for roll call anymore in the harsh Polish winter waiting hours and hours for headcount,' Hilary gave a wry smile. 'Strange isn't it, how circumstances make us view life.'

'Where you were in Auschwitz, is that where Doctor Mengele was?'

'Mengele, that vile man; no not a man, that is too kind of a word to use for him. Yes would be the answer, I'll get to him in a moment; unless you're in a hurry to leave?'

'No, I'm not pressed for time. I'd love another cuppa if one is going?'

Hilary smiled and pressed her hand on Owen's as she stood up, 'I have a slice of Battenberg going if you'd like?' Hilary was clearly disturbed by the mention of Mengele. She tried to hide her discomfort by changing the subject but she knew it was something she would have to face during her interview. Owen allowed her to continue in her own time.

'Oh go on then,' he smiled. Hilary was a generous woman and her cake tasted delightful. John wiped the corners of his mouth and licked his finger as he took the last bite.

'Where were we? That's right, Amalie! So, this little girl with the most gorgeous blue eyes looked at me, she looked right through me; she was there physically but her eyes were lost and I was fascinated from that moment on. The only real-time I saw *her* was when I had just hung up an evening gown on a clothes hanger. She came in with an armful of clothing as she normally did, saw the dress, dropped everything she had and stood there staring right up at it; her little finger stroking the fabric ever so softly. The son of the shop's owner was standing by the doorway gawping at Amalie; I could see he was going to run and squeal to his mother about what he witnessed.'

'What did you do?' Owen bit his lip.

'I grabbed him, wound a piece of rope around his neck and pulled his ear close to my mouth. I told him that if he was to mutter a word of what he saw, next time I was going to put the needle I was holding through his ear hole until it poked out the other side. Needless to say, I never saw that little boy again.

'I hadn't realised at that moment the relationship between Amalie and I would grow into a quid pro quo. My machine had skipped a thread on this one particular uniform and I was on a tight schedule so I sent it out. I didn't think anyone would notice but they did. I didn't see Amalie for three days after that. I didn't realise that when the SS noticed my error, Amalie took the blame. They beat her unconscious and how she wasn't sent to the gas chamber I will never know.'

'That was very honourable of her.'

'Yes it was; she saved me on a few occasions. She gave me her bread and soup when I contracted Typhus. Naturally, I owe my life to Amalie and that's how I came across Josef Mengele. I knew if I wasn't well enough to work within four to five days I was destined for the chambers and thanks to Amalie I struggled on. Mengele arrived at Auschwitz in 1943, and everyone knew him as the "Angel of Death". Anyone who wasn't to be sent to the gas chambers became possible targets to be experimented on, although he did have a fascination for twins, dwarves or anyone with a deformity, of course, no one knew if they fell into any of his categories. I'd prefer not to go further into detail if that's OK.'

'Was Amalie part of his experiments?'

'I think so yes, but I'm not 100% sure. I hear he's on the run. I can't say I wish him luck.'

'I just can't fathom how something of this magnitude was allowed to happen.'

'I don't think any could. I contemplated running towards the electrified fence a few times. Every morning there were more and more dead bodies along the barbed wire around the camp, but every time I stood there, the thought of leaving that little girl stopped me. We had to survive, and I kept telling myself "we will survive, we will survive".

'When the Russians approached in 1945, we were evacuated with whoever was left at Auschwitz. The Germans had left days before with other prisoners, I chose not to go and I was so thankful but we'd been without food for so long. When a Russian soldier approached me, I wrapped my arms around his neck and felt his fur hat on my skin. They gave us food but our stomachs had shrunk so small, I could only eat a few mouthfuls. Amalie just sat there ever so quiet. After that, we were on our own, not like the camps in Germany where the prisoners were cared for by the American and British soldiers. No, we had to find our own way. We were greeted with hostility in almost every country; no one was happy to see us. I really don't feel that the Russians liberated us; I think they just came across us. The war was over but the battle continued.

'Before we ended up at the orphanage, we went to a displaced person camp in Germany. It was a post-war immigration program of Allied nations. Germany and Poland were the last places I wanted to go but in reality, none of us had homes so we went along; at least we were fed. It was around this time the UNRRA became involved. They provided us with medical care, employment if we were old enough, and accommodation. But, there were too many of us and often epidemics of rickets, tuberculosis and skin infections would run rife so we were resettled in an orphanage in East Germany.

'You, and Amalie together?'

'Yes, but that was where our friendship parted ways.'

'By what means?'

'She had a look of loss in her eye, the same look she had when I first saw her. It was very chilling. When we arrived at the orphanage she became almost inaccessible and told me it was in my best interest if we stayed away from one another. I tried to reason with her but she insisted; she became quite direct.'

'I have here noted that something horrific happened at the orphanage, do you know anything about that?'

Hilary smiled, 'You know I do, you wouldn't be here and asking me that question if there was any doubt.'

'You're right.'

'The event you are referring to would be a girl called Patricia Müller. Patricia was a fascist. She would walk around goading everyone by saluting and saying, "*Heil Hitler*". When little Pete; a boy at the orphanage, laughed in her face and asked her how she can salute a dead man, she put his head in the toilet outside and flushed it while holding him under. She was a wicked girl.'

'What happened to her?'

'Mr Owen, pardon, DCI Owen, if by your coming here had been in hope that I would incriminate my only friend then you are severely mistaken.'

'She's a murderer.'

'Answer me this; How does someone get to that point where mass killing becomes morally and socially acceptable?'

'I can't answer that.'

'Neither can I, and when Amalie left, that was the last I ever saw of her. Tell me something else, why do you suspect Amalie of murder?'

'A few bodies have turned up.'

'Bodies of who?'

'War criminals, presumably Nazis, and some known gangsters.'

'Seems like to me that she's cleaning up. If it's *her* of course! I would never put Amalie down as someone to kill innocent people.'

CHAPTER 38

*I will notice how beautiful silence is when my
heart stops beating.*

Amalie sat on the chaise longue, and Charrière stared
at her in his cold disapproving way: the way he
always had just before he reprimanded her. She rolled
her eyes.

'I want to talk about you for a second. May I?'

Amalie nodded in acceptance.

'I wish I could wave a magic wand, Amalie. But I
can't, and you have a job to do.'

'No,' she huffed.

'Yes. And promise me you won't be a bad girl?'

'I promise I won't be a bad girl,' she laughed.

'I have a new assignment.'

'No, I'm not doing it.'

Charrière looked towards his hands and raised one
against Amalie's cheek. 'You're the best thing that
ever happened to me.'

'You old romantic.'

'You've come a long way, Amalie, I'm proud of
you.'

'Flattery won't get you anywhere.'

'The Brotherhood want the Krays gone.'

'I can't, sorry.'

'They have William.'

Amalie paused like she had taken a bullet to the
stomach. Mrs Campbell broke the silence by walking
in with afternoon tea.

'Tea?' Amalie asked Charrière as Mrs Campbell lowered the tray. 'Thank you, Mrs Campbell.' Amalie remained emotionally indifferent towards Charrière. He scrutinised her, looking for a weakness.

'I'd naturally ask you to remain emotionally detached, but I'm beginning to think that that is not your problem is it?'

'No.'

'And if I told you William was dead?'

'I'd say you're lying.'

'And how would you know?'

'Because Tommy Hunt is currently hanging from meat hooks. I won't be paid or bribed to kill anyone.'

Amalie recalled the murder. It wasn't carefully choreographed but more of an impromptu act. She hadn't actually planned on killing either of the Hunts. She hadn't deliberately set out to kill either of them, but Mrs Hunt's ranting tipped her off the edge. The memory played back in slow motion. As the fork sunk into Mrs Hunt's eye, Amalie picked up a bottle of Bollinger and with a downward blow it made contact with Mrs Hunt. It was only then her wailing stopped. The blood flowed over Amalie's fingers, *damn it; you've ruined a perfectly nice dress.* Her eyes gazed at each scarlet finger, entranced at the colour of her skin. She knew she should be repulsed and agitated but instead, she laughed. As she glanced over Mrs Hunt's body tutting at the spilt blood, Tommy walked in. Mrs Hunt had just been an act of spontaneity, but Tommy had it coming. She grabbed at the table knife and eyed it like it were solid gold before lunging it towards Tommy; it gave Amalie a moment of pleasure to inflict pain with something so cheap and meaningless. Even though mass-produced, the knife slipped into his chest like butter. It was a matter of irony the butcher was to die by a butcher's main instrument, a knife. But she couldn't let him die yet.

'Where's William?'

Tommy took Amalie to the last location where William was known to be alive. She twisted the blade to make him scream whilst sinking it deeper.

The abandoned warehouse had metal racks suspended from the ceiling and various other apparatus. The foreboding abandoned meat factory wasn't somewhere Amalie wanted to spend any more time than necessary, and as they walked through the haunting corridors, Amalie caught sight of the grim machinery, a few reminders of what must have gone on there.

The lower level was structurally intact with rows of hooks hanging from some sort of conveyor which would have wound its way around the ceiling. The musty scent of rotting wood and the ghostly aroma of the animals that were here were a haunting reminder of past operations.

'I want you to realise, I never wanted any of this; this life. But you couldn't leave me alone. You couldn't leave *us* alone. And one by one you're taking any last bit of humanity I may have had.'

Tommy laughed at Amalie, even with a knife protruding from his chest.

'Humanity? You wouldn't be in this job if you had any of that, Amalie. Yes, I know who you are. We all know who you are. Oh, and if you think you're going to see William again, think again, Sunshine. Charlie takes good care of his friends.'

Amalie reached forward and twisted the knife a final time. Tommy's body convulsed. She slipped a yellow coverall on, zipped it up the front, tied his feet and hoisted him into the air. The chain grated as it moved along the pulley, and she stopped once his head cleared the floor. He swung back and forth suspended from the ceiling and the blood slowly trickled from his open wound towards his face. She took out her chiv from her carry bag, and at the sight of the blade, he squealed like a pig. She laughed, '"Sometimes the lambs slaughter the butcher".'

X

BERKSHIRE, ENGLAND

CHAPTER 39

Do you know how you caught me?

John looked at his reflection in the mirror and cut himself on the side of the face with his razor. He edged forwards to look closer at the blood that oozed from the wound. He pressed his skin to feel the sting and hoped he could understand Amalie's thoughts and violent disposition better.

Why had Amalie kept John alive? She had so many opportunities to do him harm, and if she had been your garden variety sequence killer, she would have derived great pleasure in bringing him to harm. Instead she teased him and taunted him. Amalie mocked John. He asked himself, *why didn't he finish her when he had the opportunity?*

Identifying Amalie Keller as the slayer of fugitive war criminals gave DCI John Owen something momentous to think about. He had become by default a go-between Amalie and MI6.

Since the death of his father, Owen's life had changed dramatically. His mother kept him in forever damnation as his resemblance to his father was uncanny. His co-workers in the Staffordshire Police had a look of wariness, and he was rarely invited to social gatherings. He was a lone wolf, his movements choreographed motions. The other MI6 agents told Owen he was made an off the grid agent far too early, and he was known to generally be hard to handle.

London had its fair share of dangerous wildcards

but this one always seemed to be one step ahead; Owen suspected a mole to be working out of MI6.

London's underground had been growing in the shadows for years but their world was sealed. The Kray twins were protected by a mafia-esque circle which combined powerful cronies in the establishment and protection rackets that the Krays had bullied their way into. They were in cahoots with the American mafia, and together shared control of London with their rivals – The Richardson gang. In the mid to late 60s, MI6 and MI5 had their hands full. Both Reggie and Ronnie Kray became murderers. Now kingpins of the underworld, the underground feared for their protection rackets. Known celebrities such as Frank Sinatra and British pin-ups such as Barbara Windsor were photographed beside them. In Ronnie's words, "we were fucking untouchable".

In the circus of it all, a lone female assassin was at the bottom of the pile. Scotland Yard was finding bodies dumped here, there and everywhere. They had Kray written all over them. Jack "The Hat" McVitie was known to authorities and had acted as an enforcer and hitman with links to the Krays. He wound up dead in 1967. The plan never was to kill McVitie, but Reggie lost it. Whilst arguing with McVitie and trying to show him that messing with the Krays was not a smart move, Reggie pulled out a gun and tried to shoot him in the head. When the gun jammed, he stabbed him multiple times in the stomach, face and neck. It was an act of such violence that other gangsters were horrified. Minor members of The Firm collected the body, wrapped it in an eiderdown and left it outside St. Mary's Church, Rotherhithe. When the Kray twins discovered where the body had been left, they ordered the immediate removal because of its close proximity to another known gangster. The body was never found. But, McVitie was just the beginning. Reggie's trail of blood would eventually lead to the Kray's downfall. McVitie was stabbed to death because the Krays believed one of their associates was going to turn informant and ordered McVitie to assassinate him. He failed. But, before McVitie, a member of the Firm's rival gang, George Cornell of The Richardson Gang, was murdered. Scrap metal dealers *and* criminals wound up dead.

On the 9th of March, 1966, Ronnie Kray and his right-hand man, Ian Barrie, walked into the Blind Beggar Pub in Whitechapel. Their driver waited outside in his white MK1 Cortina. The history of the Blind Beggar confessed to hosting its fair share of villains. Before WW1, the Blind Beggar had been known as the meeting place for a pickpocket gang, and in 1904, "Bulldog" Wallace stabbed another man in the eye with an umbrella. *"No one saw nuffink!"* Unlike Wallace, Kray hadn't received a cheer when he entered the Blind Beggar. Barrie shot two bullets towards the ceiling to notify everyone of their arrival. Ronnie Kray had been informed that George Cornell was drinking in the pub. When Ronnie arrived, he saw Cornell was sitting with two friends at one end of the bar. An elderly gentleman sat at the other reading a newspaper and watching the television. When Cornell saw Ronnie approach he sarcastically commented as a warning to the waitress, "Well look who's here". Whilst the friends walked away, Ronnie took out a 9mm and shot Cornell through the head at close range. Kray and his right-hand man left him bleeding on the floor of the Blind Beggar. An ambulance was called, and he was transferred to Maida Vale Hospital. Roughly two hours later, Cornell died.

No one wanted any involvement that would lead to the Krays being put away. The old man claimed, "I hate the sight of blood, particularly my own". And the waitress said she hadn't seen who did it. A year later when Reggie had murdered McVitie, a member of the gang claimed that, "when Reggie was stabbing Jack, his liver popped out and they had to flush it down the toilet". How much of that is true, no one knows. Detective Chief Superintendent Leonard "Nipper" Read of Scotland Yard had been promoted to Murder Squad, and his first assignment had been to bring down the Krays. By 1967, he managed to gather enough evidence but frequently came up against their "wall of silence." It was two years later that the Kray twins were arrested for the two murders. With a team of nearly one hundred armed police officers, they managed to arrest the twins and twenty-four other members of the Firm, but it wasn't until 1969 that they were convicted. Each brother was sentenced to life imprisonment with a non-parole period of thirty years. But for every villain that was put behind bars, there were two more willing to take their place.

Owen hadn't been involved directly in the investigation of the systematic extortion and fraud that had been occurring for over a decade with the Krays, but he used what evidence he could to learn about London's underground – who was running it and what was going on; who hated who, that kind of thing. He wondered what information would become useful, but his business was to prepare for the eventuality of Keller's next appearance. Amalie was brilliant at concealment. There was no particular order to the hundreds of pieces of paper and newspaper articles he had collected. He hadn't known the exact order of events until after the events had occurred. Among the papers was a receipt from the *Hôtel de passé* in Paris where a known member of France's organised crime group *Corso-Marseillais* was found dead. The receipt was for a bottle of the most perfect burgundy, a classic Pinot Noir which happened to be one of the most sought after wines around – how exquisite the Château Lafite 1787 must have tasted. Amalie clearly wasn't a woman who denied herself anything. Owen wondered if she had enjoyed the Caviar too. It was something he had never tried.

Learning of William's disappearance from Mrs Campbell made Owen uneasy. He had grown fond of William in the last decade and foolishly believed Amalie would have been at the residence when he arrived. With bodies turning up from both gangs in London and the disappearance of William, it became evident that Amalie had taken matters into her own hands. *The Brotherhood surely wouldn't be happy with that?*

The discovery of the corpse of Jimmy Costa – a lieutenant of one of London's most notorious gangs showed Owen that Amalie was working up the chain. The Krays hadn't been of importance, she was after the unknowns. If you were a real gangster, nobody would know who you were and carrying out an assassination on some gangster from South London because he called Ronnie "a fat poof" wouldn't have entertained her in the slightest. The fame they craved ensured they would be targeted by the police; they staged their crimes so they had a guaranteed audience and yet foolishly believed their men were loyal to them. Those were the men who guaranteed the Kray's downfall. Amalie stayed away from the limelight.

Whilst the gang members were in prison, Detective Chief Superintendent Leonard "Nipper" Read secretly interviewed each of the arrested and offered each member of the gang a deal if they testified against the others. It led to a name; Tommy Hunt.

Tommy Hunt owned a private abattoir that had been under investigation and was temporarily closed due to foot-and-mouth disease being found in cattle that were waiting to be slaughtered. Foot-and-mouth had reached its peak back in 1957. It still affected England and Wales but mostly in the North West, and workers in the meat industry had a restriction on animal movements within a ten-mile radius.

After he stomped through the rain, Owen arrived at the abattoir. His eyes travelled over the carcass that was Tommy Hunt. His body was strung up and different shades of red-streaked his pale skin. He dangled from a hook and his feet cramped together suggested he suffered.

Owen flinched and when he turned around the corner, Amalie was standing there, rigid and aloof.

As Owen fixated on his target; Amalie wiped her blade clean. When he shouted, 'Freeze!' she answered,

'What took you so long?'

He instinctively reached for his gun in his shoulder holster, but he didn't draw it. It was more to reassure himself that it was there, should he need it and if the situation called for a duel.

Amalie toyed with the knife; she could see the fear in Owen's eyes. He didn't want to kill her; did he have a choice? Was this the moment he could see a psychopath learning to have feelings? Or was it the moment that he started to lose the parts of himself that made him who he was?

'Please, come with me, just you and me?' he pleaded as he pointed his gun between her eyes.

'Come on, John, you know the rules of the game. You've been playing it long enough,' she smirked.

'You don't have to do this.'

'Speak for yourself, or have you lost your nerve?'

'I want to do the right thing.'

'Then take the bloody shot,' she growled. 'Come on, John. How long are we going to dance together?'

'I know William is missing and I'll find him, but this isn't the way.'

'It's the only way I know.' Amalie took the knife and placed it under her chin and laughed. '"Through every city shall he hunt her down, until he shall have driven her back to Hell, therefrom whence envy first did let her loose".'

'Therefore I think and judge it for thy best Thou follow me, and I will be thy guide, And lead thee hence through the eternal place".'

'NO!' she screamed. 'We've been here before you and I and we both know you're not going to shoot me.'

'Not if I don't have to.'

'Sometimes when you love someone you'll do crazy things.'

'You don't know the meaning of the word.'

'Don't speak to me like that, John, I like you but I'm not sure I like you that much. I do know the meaning of the word, you're mine.'

'I don't belong to anyone. Turn yourself in and I'll make sure you stay safe.'

'Never!' As the knife pricked at Amalie's skin, Owen's gun went off.

'Are you going to shoot me?'

'Yes, if I have to.'

'I have to find William.'

'There's a right way and a wrong way,' Owen answered pointing his gun. 'This time I'm not aiming for your knees.'

'OK, say I trust you and you take me in. Would you thus trust me to do one more thing?'

'You're not harming anyone else, Amalie.'

Amalie laughed as she slowly backed away from Tommy Hunt's hanging body. She pivoted and ran towards the exit. Owen aimed and shot but he missed. *Did he miss intentionally?*

Her silk scarf offered an uplifting hint of glamour among the surroundings; it evoked that Grace Kelly glamour in 'To catch a thief' with Cary Grant, and was a wearable piece of art. As Amalie ran it unravelled and wafted in the air like a blossom in the wind. He reached to grab it before it dropped into the bloody puddle.

CHAPTER 40

"He who is unable to live in society, or who has no need because he is sufficient for himself, must be either a beast or a god." Aristotle.

Graham Young had been admitted to Broadmoor in 1961 as a bright 14-year-old child. His father had purchased him a chemistry set when he was just eleven thinking he was interested in science – what he was really interested in was poison, and he'd experiment with his family by putting Strychnine in the Sunday roast to observe what would happen. He kept a log of the gradually increasing dosages. He eventually killed his stepmother, and the strychnine permanently damaged the internal organs of his father and sister.

He was eventually caught and sent to Broadmoor for ten years for his crimes. Whilst in Broadmoor he placed Harpic toilet bowl cleaner in the tea urn and thus resulted in patients suffering from internal organ damage. He got a job working at a photographic laboratory in Hertfordshire – ironically the only industrial unit in England that used Thallium, a rare metal poison that fascinated Young. His room at Broadmoor had been covered with pictures of Hitler and Swastikas, but the doctors hadn't been aware of the warning signs. Amalie had been grateful Young was no longer at Broadmoor; she hadn't quite imagined her demise would be at the hand of a Teacup Poisoner for she did enjoy a nice brew now and then.

Although she did admire him as a gifted chemist, having a passion for poison is one thing, but having one for Nazis didn't bode well with Amalie. If he were to openly read Mein Kampf and speak about the virtues of Hitler in front of her, she'd have to cut out his tongue. Amalie was thankful he had been moved to HM Prison in Parkhurst – Isle of Wight. The act would not have been a good start to her rehabilitation.

Some might even say that for the mentally ill the Holocaust never ended, and even though some twenty-odd years later, there are still sometimes screams of "The Nazis are coming". Amalie wasn't the only patient in Broadmoor that had connections to the tragedy of World War Two. Some patients even refused to shower because it would remind them of the gas chambers, and others would stockpile food in their pillowcases for fear of hunger.

Like Amalie, many survivors remained frozen in time, and as life continued the survivors became "the forgotten people". These are the ones that have been left behind, the people that fall between the cracks, that can't forget the past and cannot move forward. The shadow of the death camps is never far away, and even for those with their sanity relatively intact, it is suspected it could take years perhaps decades for them to breach their silence. Most of the survivors at Broadmoor don't speak at all, introverted and unresponsive. Amalie would see the same people flumped in front of a TV looking aimlessly into the distance.

When an audio message that was purported to have

come from outer space was broadcasted during an ITN news bulletin announcing the destiny of the human race and a disaster to affect "your world and the beings on other worlds around you" Amalie looked for a response, but they just stared, sucking hard into their cigarettes.

The Independent Broadcasting Authority confirmed it was the first time a transmission like this had been made and speculation arose that it had originated from an Alien race; strange how this alien spoke with a British accent.

Like Amalie, details of their haunted pasts were revealed in their behaviour. One inmate, a fellow Hungarian with a deep surly expression, had survived the Mauthausen concentration camp. When questioned by a psychiatrist about World War Two, he just looked away and quivered. Reminiscing is impossible. Amalie overheard Dr Harlow talking to visitors once, stating that "this place functions as a nursing home for people with cognitive limitations who cannot live among the general community" at which she just rolled her eyes.

MI6 was having a different kind of celebration. Amalie Keller had been caught.

'I'd like you to do a psychological profile of Amalie Keller,' Harrison said.

A brief silence followed. John Owen stared at Harrison 'Keller the killer?' he asked.

'Yes.'

'I'm appreciative of the opportunity, but I'm left wondering why me? I'm hardly qualified.'

'No one else wants to. They aren't *available*,'

Harrison stated. 'I don't expect her to cooperate, but she's in isolation and may appreciate the companionship.'

Harrison took a swill of coffee and sat back at his desk. 'If she won't talk, just give me a straight report; your observations, behaviour, her room, that kind of thing. Be careful speaking to the media; they love anything to do with Broadmoor, more so than The Beatles.

'Dr Harlow, head of Broadmoor will go over the physical procedures upon your arrival. Please do not deviate from them. It's not *just* her in there remember.'

'I *do* know her.'

Harrison smiled at him. 'Just remember what she is.'

'And that is?'

'A savage. She's now in isolation because in the medium secure unit she sharpened the handle of her toothbrush and tried to stab another inmate in the face.'

'Right.'

'And take no notice of what Harlow tells you about Keller. Apparently, she jerked him around well and truly. He made a right twat of himself on the four 'o'clock news when he boasted about a Hansom Tiling being a new name on a case.'

'Hansom?'

'Yeah, apparently she called him a Night soil man.'

'Which is what exactly?'

'A gong farmer; faecal sludge to you and me. She basically outed him in public as the person that takes out the shit.'

'Ouch.'

'I think he had it coming. He's been trying to fuck Keller ever since she's been in there.'

'He's brave.'

'Or stupid.'

Broadmoor Hospital houses some of the country's most notorious killers. Targeted with intense criticism, it's primarily a hospital with one obligation to the public and that was to ensure no one escaped. It had an atmosphere of hopelessness, and patients asked daily when they were going to get out. No one had that answer.

Many patients were socially inadequate; they weren't wanted. It's as simple as that. Society doesn't deem them "normal", and often patients with no psychiatric reason to be there, only that they couldn't "cope", were dumped by relatives. And yet some of the country's most violent criminals would call it home.

If someone escaped, a siren would sound, and it would strike terror into even the hardest of criminals. Uncertainty is a fear factor here and rarely anyone gets along.

Broadmoor was a name that brought most people to shiver. Was it a prison, or was it a hospital? It's easy to label someone as a monster, lock them in a cell and throw away the key.

Just forty miles from the centre of London, Broadmoor, first built as a lunatic asylum for the criminally insane, boasts a 12ft wall and an institution for the mentally disturbed.

Dr Harlow, fifty-two years old and head of

Broadmoor, had a long mahogany desk which boasted very little, not even a pen. John Owen approached him while he remained seated.

'DCI Owen? They told me I was to expect you. May I see your credentials?' Owen handed over his badge.

'We've had quite a few officers over the years, but never have I come across one so unqualified. You must be something quite special,' he said without moving.

Owen had been informed that Amalie had taken a dislike to Dr Harlow. Owen could see why.

'I didn't get a say in the matter,' Owen answered.

'Well this won't take long, she's ever so uncooperative. I'm not sure why they sent you to be perfectly honest.'

'I understand from my superior you will brief me with the physical procedures?'

'Yes, it won't take long. Follow me.' Dr Harlow stood and brushed past Owen.

'Will you be available while I'm interviewing Keller? It's just I may need to go over a few questions with you during her interview, about her answers and her body language.'

'I'll catch up with you afterwards. I have a few assignments I need to complete.'

'I was under the impression we had an appointment?'

'Yes, but you're not here to see me. Oh, before you go in, I'll need your jacket and any other personal items please.'

'Certainly.'

'The guard will need to pat you down. Are you

carrying?'
    'No.'

    Owen followed Dr Harlow down the dark corridor.
It had as much personality as a rubber duck. The floor
was a dark grey, the rooms were windowless, no real
light and the doors were without handles. A cheap
analogue clock ticked. They say there is time, and
then there's Broadmoor time. It ticked loudly on a
nearby wall in tune with each step Owen made
towards Amalie's room. He could hear the moans and
screams from adjacent patients, and he was glad it
wasn't them he had come to visit. He was glad he
didn't have to show any sympathy, sympathy he
didn't have. Owen recoiled at the sound of the gate
closing behind him and the guard locking it shut.
    'Hey Harlow, I tried shaving the crack of 'ma ass
once. Ever tried that? The hair was gettin' too long
and shit was sticking to it, so I shaved it. I scalped my
ass and ended up expecting to see half a hole on the
floor,' an inmate shouted. Owen's brows raised and
the corner of his mouth lifted as if to smile.
    Dr Harlow walked a few feet ahead still instructing
the procedures.
    'Amalie has caused quite the stir among the other
inmates during her stay,' he mumbled looking back at
Owen.
    'Why is that?'
    'Well, it's not that often we have a female
sociopath arrive through our doors; a pretty one at
that. Harrison has been very clever using you to do
the interview hasn't he?'
    'What do you mean?'

'Didn't he tell you? It's the only name she has mentioned since she's been here "Owen".'

'No, he didn't say.'

Another inmate grabbed the bars and pressed his face between them and startled Owen, 'Did you just say Amalie? I warned her not to wake the monster,' he pointed between his legs, 'it's like an elephant's trunk when it wakes up. It can pick up a currant bun from five feet away.' The inmate winked at Owen.

'Well, here we are.' Dr Harlow stated. 'Do not touch her. Do not pass her anything. If you have to show her something, hold it up at least three feet from the bars. Do not accept anything from her, if you need any assistance ring the bell. Understood?' Dr Harlow pointed to a bell hanging beside the cell.

'Understood.'

'I'll be in my office but the orderly down the corridor will assist you.'

Dr Harlow sensed he wasn't going to find out what the interview was about and left without looking back.

John Owen looked down the corridor, the last inmate had been a few doors back and he was entering solitary confinement. A light lit the end cell, it was twenty feet away.

The staff were reminded daily of the security, at least four attacks occurred every week. It was a common practice among such violent inmates.

Cranfield ward was notorious for where Broadmoor kept its most violent patients and where some inmates are so ill, it takes six members of staff to open a single door.

After the escape of child murderer John Straffen in

1952, Broadmoor installed a system where any other patient that decided to make the great escape thereafter, thirteen sirens would howl like a wartime air raid in nearby villages. Straffen escaped whilst on cleaning duty, he had climbed onto a shed and descended the other side. He sauntered into a village and strangled a five-year-old girl riding her bike. Locals thought his behaviour odd, and called the police. He'd been out less than twenty-four hours.

Dr Harlow described Amalie as a prized asset and a schizophrenic capable of extreme, unprovoked violence. *Do you believe that?*

CHAPTER 41

"I hope this fellow is not going to be late"

'Well hello, John.'

'Hello, Amalie.'

John looked good, he always looked good. She guessed he did know her after all. The only person that really did. He was the only one that believed she shouldn't be sat here in a straight jacket dosed up and spaced out on a cocktail of chemicals. He looked at her as if disappointed, and she fought the urge to tell him about the other day when she ran naked down the corridor, because she fancied a toss and tumble with security. Somehow, she didn't feel he shared the moment. Amalie longed so much for human touch but somehow the psych nurses who pushed her *face down and injected her in the arse*, didn't quite match up to expectations. She would have to reconsider whether to tell him, maybe after he's finished interviewing her? They might share a moment of laughter?

His questions bored her, *when did he become so boring?* Was he following orders?

'John?' she interrupted.

'Yes, Amalie?'

'Just because I survived, doesn't mean I could live.'

'Do you have any remorse for what you did to those people?'

'Those people are murderers, and if I wasn't sat here I'd be with Skorzeny as we speak,' she huffed.

'I hear he's dying of lung cancer in Madrid.'

'So karma comes round for everyone eventually,' she shrugged.

Owen stayed with Amalie for just over an hour. *Did she deserve to be in here?* He remembered the sign he had passed coming in.

Please ensure the gate is closed.
SECURITY IS EVERYONE'S
RESPONSIBILITY

'I'm happy to be kept in solitary – away from those animals anyway. Did you hear Robert Maudsley a few years back tortured a paedo before garrotting him? Staff said that, when they were let into the cell, the inmate's skull had been cracked open like a boiled egg and a spoon was hanging out with part of his brain missing. He's further down the hall – in solitary like me if you fancied having a chat?'

'I'm just here to see you.'

'You always did make me feel special, John,' she smiled. 'Sure, they offer the finest health cover, the best psychiatric care and security forever needs an upgrade. They've just put up razor wire around the perimeter, oh how Dr William Chester Minor would have loved that! He could have cut off his own penis while trying to escape instead of using a pen knife!'

The patients that come to Broadmoor would have committed horrendous crimes, but *they,* too, can often be victims. It's easy to see somebody as either a perpetrator or a victim but it's much more difficult to understand that someone might be both.

'They think I'm locked up, but if I wanted to leave,

I'd just tie a few sheets together and hop over the wall,' Amalie remarked. Owen didn't say much. He observed, took notes and listened more.

Amalie possessed a cold and brutal nature that was hidden by her innocent exterior. She happily would live outside law and order and lacked any moral code. She'd kill with flamboyance and without conscience, but she was also playful and vulnerable. She was very troubled. Her desire for revenge had overwhelmed her, and her ego allowed her to believe she was invincible.

'What do I get from your visit, John?'

'Nothing, I'm not here to play your perverse game of quid pro quo, Amalie.'

'Perverse? Now we're getting somewhere,' she smiled.

That evening Owen contemplated his report. He sat in his living room watching the fire burning under the mantelpiece. He couldn't breathe and neither could he hear his heart throbbing at the anxiety of the day's events. The once beautiful wooden log was now cracked and disintegrating under the reign of terror. He watched as it burned, and the smell drifted throughout his home. The fire danced, so unyielding, it hissed and spat feverishly at him, enticing him and he reached inside immersed in the temptation, and like a snake with its vicious fangs, it bit back.

Steve Harrison hadn't been pleased, but not surprised to hear that Keller the killer had been uncooperative, and that Owen had nothing to report and he relieved Owen of the assignment.

Though Owen's mission hadn't been completed.

While he watched the fire, John withdrew a piece of paper where he'd written a name, a name Amalie had given him. As he read the name aloud, he recalled her last words as he walked away from her cell.

'But, humans by nature, John, their behaviour will remain unmanageable forever.'

Charrière had been apprehended outside the Theatre Royal, Haymarket that was receiving a rapturous reception. He got caught selling Black Market tickets for £5; that was five times more than the original price. Avid fans would pay whatever he asked to be a part of the premiere screening of the highly anticipated performance. Getting nicked for a petty crime is a far cry from the preconceived mob boss Owen was led to believe, but then an overconfident adversary is prone to carelessness.

In December, 1980, Charrière was transferred to Rampton Secure Hospital. Unable to adapt to the forced medication, and being in the companionship of disturbed and dangerous patients, Charrière attempted to strangle child rapist Gary Bishop. Charrière was seized just as Bishop was giving out his death rattle.

'You can't keep me here,' Charrière begged. 'They're nuts.' Charrière reported witnessing inmates at Rampton run into walls and knock themselves unconscious. One even tried to eat himself by constantly biting his arms and fingers. Charrière wanted out, and he'd do anything to make it happen.

Owen visited the Hospital whilst Charrière was on a ten-day hunger strike to aid his transfer request.

'Where's William?' Owen got right to the point.

'They certify me mad because of whom I'm associated with.' Charrière changed the subject.

'Where's William?'

'William? Sorry, don't know a William,' Charrière shrugged.

Owen slammed his fist on the table.

'I've heard Peter Dinsdale is due to arrive at Rampton.'

'DAFT PETER? Get out of here,' Charrière laughed.

'You've heard of him?'

'Sure, I've heard of the horrifying Hull murderer. Didn't he call himself Bruce Lee?'

'So, I've heard,' Owen was getting somewhere.

'You're locking me up in here with the likes of people that call themselves after a Legendary Kung Fu martial artist? Where's the sanity in that? This system is just as crazy as Pete,' Charrière shook his head.

'So...'

'So, what?'

'William?'

Charrière sat still looking DCI Owen in the eyes. He knew if he wanted out, this might be his opportunity.

'Say I know a William, what's in it for me?'

'Well, you might not have to worry about sleeping next to an arsonist that burnt children in their sleep!'

'Pete's crazy, but I'm not afraid of him.'

'He stands trial next month to twenty-six counts of murder and eleven counts of arson.'

'And?'

'What do you want, Charrière?'

'I want out.'

'I can try to get you a reduced sentence if you

cooperate. It's the best I can do. My hands are tied.'

'I can give you information on the Yorkshire Ripper.'

'And William!'

'And William...'

There it was. It was never understood how many pies Charrière had his fingers in, but information leading to the closure of one of the country's most prolific cases was sure to lead Owen in a good light. He took the deal.

CHAPTER 42

"The measure of a man is what he does with power" Plato

By the 1980s, Margaret Thatcher had already won the election and was now Prime Minister. England was convulsed by a social revolution with great innovation in pop music. The likes of David Bowie started to experiment with synthesisers and new technology that was sure to change the way music was made. The news was circulating that the Prince of Wales had proposed to his new love interest, Diana, and they were soon to be married.

As Owen walked with his hands in the pockets of his long trench coat, he thought about the events of the last few days. He struggled to concentrate as he stalked the night streets of London, absorbing its magic and mystery. At night, London had fewer people wandering the streets; he could see distinctive architectural lines and shadows with just a single light source coming from a street lamp. The sounds were eerie; a scurrying, a sniffling, a squeak and dustbins banged. The sounds combined with the smell of hundreds of discarded takeaway meals down dark alleyways where the darkness was a solid black mass made Owen want to walk faster. He hated rats. Even with a quick pace and determination, he wasn't exempt from suspicion and invited the impression he was on the run from something or someone. Owen remembered when his mother used to read him night time stories. Charles Dickens, in a book titled The Uncommercial Traveller, chapter 10 Shy Neighbours, explained how, "walking is of two kinds: one, straight on end to a definite goal at a round pace;" and another type was "objectless, loitering, and purely vagabond".

For Owen, walking streets like these was usually in the pursuit of the deviant or dispossessed person. Let's be honest, who walked the streets alone at night? The unfortunate? The mad? The bad? There was something sinister about the streets of London at night and the few people that passed him were in a rush, a rush to go where? Why was everyone in a rush? Head down and pay no attention to anyone. Maybe it gave them a sense of anonymity. If Dickens' theory was correct, that walking is a form of travel from point A to point B, then, surely his second theory was that there was no point at all; thus night walking was illogical and pointless. To walk the streets at night where most of us are asleep in preparation for the next day, then, quintessentially, night walking was indeed "objectless, loitering and vagabond".

Owen adopted the same anonymity technique. He walked along the cobbled streets between buildings that loomed at him either side, and he thought that the brick walls had been a romantic feature, but soon they became daunting as the vines crept up and cast shadows like Scarecrows.

As Owen stood at the pub's entrance, he paused before turning the handle. What was he to find? Why had he been sent here? As he opened the door, the cigarette smoke billowed out into the bitter streets of

London. The patrons inside were laughing and swilling their drinks. If they had been sober, the brutality of their conversation may have ended up in a fistfight instead of laughter.

One of the drunkards at the bar lifted his head in a drunken stupor and shouted towards Owen.

'Ow 'bout a 'rink old chap?'

Owen smiled back and nodded his head as he approached the bar. A man stood behind the bar drying glasses.

'What can I get 'ya?'

'I'm looking for someone by the name of Frank Wilson?' Owen furrowed his brow as he asked the bartender who fixed a stare into Owen's eyes.

'We don't want any trouble here. I don't need the rozzers sniffing 'round, it's not good for business if 'ya get 'ma drift?'

'He's not in any trouble and I'd prefer to keep my presence here unknown,' Owen answered.

The barman gave a wry smile and lifted his head nodding it in a backwards motion to gesture Frank Wilson was sitting in a dark corner of the pub. As Owen approached, he saw the man sitting alone with his hands cupped around a glass.

'What took you so long?' Wilson asked.

DCI John Owen sat beside Wilson and he smiled, unable to answer the question. Wilson spoke again. 'I always knew you were a good Detective, but now I believe you are a great Detective. I just thought you'd find me quicker than that.'

'We were all worried about you, William.'

'Please, if these guys find out who I am, I'll be beaten to a pulp.'

'It's not that bad,' Owen laughed.

'How is she?' William asked curiously.

'Safe,' Owen answered reassuringly.

'I think we have long established that, it's not her safety we have to be careful of.'

'Amalie is in isolation,' Owen stated.

'Is there any chance of parole?'

'To be honest, I don't know. How did you do it Will......son?

William took a sip from his glass and began.

'When I discovered it was Charrière who had been behind my kidnapping, I realised he didn't have Amalie's best interest at heart. And to be fair, he was getting a little too big for his boots. I knew I couldn't have him bumped off, that would always come and bite me in the arse, but isn't it fitting he'd wind up in the loony house for a petty crime? I knew Charrière prided himself more than to be associated with the likes of nutters, and that the only officer that would be bothered to continue an investigation of my whereabouts would be you.'

'That's one hell of a risk,' Owen gasped.

'Nothing ventured, nothing gained Owen.'

'So, what about Amalie? Where does she fit in all of this?'

'Amalie. I will try to keep alive for as long as I shall live. She's the only surviving family I have. Her mother died at Auschwitz and my brother died because of the bloody war. I just cannot fathom what that girl has been through. Her story is a testament to the brutality that humans are capable of. She may be a murderer herself, but her story is just one story, a story six million other people cannot tell. She was and always shall be a witness to mass murder. Wouldn't that drive you a little crazy?'

'Yes. "Thou shalt not be a victim, thou shalt not be a perpetrator, but, above all, thou shalt not be a bystander."'

CHAPTER 43

End Game

'Let me run, John. Why don't you let me run?' Those were the last words Owen remembered from Amalie whilst he read the headlines of the Daily Mirror.

It was early morning and Owen sat outside his little slice of heaven; the corner coffee shop. He liked to get there just after 08.00 am, after the coffee grinder but before the jabbering staff arrived. The shop had that aromatic coffee bean swirl in the air and as he sat down, he was just in time to see those first sun rays that indicated the day had just begun.

'Usual?' asked the waiter, and Owen nodded as he opened the pages of the Daily Mirror. He gave the paper a quick shake as he propped it in front of him just as his coffee arrived. Owen would rarely start his day without the daily paper, without fail he was sure to find an article that would rub him up the wrong way. Like an addiction, the provocative titles were designed to agitate the middle class, full of drama and controversy and something gloomy to keep the cynics content. Owen sipped on his tepid bitter coffee and pursed his lips, and he squinted his eyes as he swallowed a large gulp. It tasted more like boiled dirty water.

As he perused a copy of the newspaper, Owen laid the paper down to turn the page and a headline caught his eye.

PRISONER ESCAPES BROADMOOR

His eyes widened and he knocked his coffee to the floor. A waiter ran over, dived towards the floor to grab the cup as it smashed, but Owen didn't see nor hear the waiter, he saw only the headline. *It couldn't be?* He read on.

"Prisoner escaped from Broadmoor Hospital in Berkshire by scaling an 18-foot inner wall using a grappling hook attached to a makeshift rope."

Police have set up roadblocks in Berkshire, Surrey and Hampshire, and people have been warned not to approach the suspect who is described as five feet five inches (1.68 metres) tall and 8 stone (51 kg) in weight.

The prisoner recently wrote to Home Secretary Mark Shore protesting that Mr Shore had blocked their release despite a favourable psychologist's report.

A police spokesman said it could be that the prisoner - who they believe had outside assistance - had escaped to prove a point.

Owen closed his eyes in angst. The truth was, it proved embarrassingly easy for dangerous patients to escape. The ageing staff were well past their sell-by-date professionally and more than likely not overpaid for their ever-demanding job.

The newspaper was splashed with headlines and assumptions on the escapee and their horrific story that entailed. *"Was it Sutcliff?"* One reporter asked, *"So soon after being incarcerated under Section 47 of the Mental Health Act that passed in 1983?"*

The media were like a plague of locusts, and like sharks, once they smelt the slightest hint of an escaped prisoner; they were swarming and went into a veritable feeding frenzy.

Owen placed his mouth into his hand and rubbed it gently. He recalled the moment he had Amalie in his line of shot and wondered if he would be able to let her go a second time. For sure, MI6 would be back knocking on his door now knowing their most prized convict was once again on the loose. Amalie was the best contract killer he had ever come across, and she didn't do it for the money. She had enough money to last her a lifetime several times over. She'd become a ghost and eventually would make her way round the globe taking out drug dealers, mobsters, rapists, and basically anyone that pissed her off. If she could get paid along the way, she'd take it; after all, it did give her protection, from one side for a while at least.

Wherever Amalie went, bodies followed; did John Owen really want to get involved? Hilary had illuminated the fact she would be surprised if Amalie actually killed an innocent being, and Amalie's list of victims had been perpetrators of one crime or another.

He reminisced about the silk scarf he had kept from Amalie; did she notice it was missing? And he touched his lips recalling how he'd stroke it across them inhaling her scent.

'Thanks, Pete, for the coffee, but maybe a little warmer next time?' Owen left some loose change on the table as he headed home. *Where have you disappeared to now, Amalie?*

Owen packed a few items of clothing into an overnight carry case. He had a hunch that Amalie had gone to France, Paris to be exact. A witness outside the Hunt's Mayfair home on the night of the murder had stated that the Hunts were expecting a French actress that evening, and bragged how she had told them about a play she was in at the Théâtre de l'Athénée in Paris.

Owen's hunch paid off, and as he walked down the centre of the street under the darkness of night, he saw the Eiffel Tower standing proudly like a metal skeleton, a wrought iron lattice on the Champ de Mars in Paris. Other than the darkness and himself, all that existed was a chill wind whose bite he could feel through his coat. He tucked his hands into his pockets, lowering his head as his blood ran cold through his veins. As he stood outside the majestic 1930s building, he watched from the darkness of the street.

He withdrew his camera and its telephoto lens from his pocket and held it up to his eye.

Through it, he watched as the light ignited at one of the windows.

Owen didn't dare move; he tried to not even breathe. He was frozen, and he could feel his heart pounding heavily within his chest. He drew in a deep breath in the cold air and steadily released the warm mist from his mouth as he felt his heart thud.

The hairs along his arms stood, and chills descended his spine. He could hear his heart beating, a cacophonous thrumming with an intolerable pain. As he lowered the camera, he whispered, 'Dear God.'

Lifting the camera to his eye once again, he held his breath as he snapped away. A woman brushed past the glass. It was Amalie.

Amalie sat on the edge of her bed with damp hair that trailed down her back. She opened her side drawer and her hand happened upon her silk scarf that she had lost some time ago. It smelled as fresh and clean as the day she bought it. As she took it out the drawer and held it in front of her, a note fell; on it in elegant handwriting addressed simply to "Amalie". It read:

Dear Amalie,

I trust you are well after your stay at Broadmoor. I'm afraid you misplaced this during one of our final encounters, I felt obliged to return it. I took the liberty of having it cleaned; I hope that was all right.

It was lovely to see you again. Until next time, Amalie

Forget-me-not
Yours truly,
O

Amalie knew instantly who wrote the letter, and it flashed through her mind. She had never known Owen to be dishonest nor untruthful and she knew the moment she read, *"Until next time"* that he would be following her once again. The thought didn't make her uncomfortable at all, and as she looked out the window, she set her wine glass aside. A tear rolled down her cheek and Owen pressed the button to capture the shot. He saw her standing by the window looking out into the darkness, a towel wrapped across the top of her breasts and her dark damp hair trailing across her shoulders. He saw her holding the scarf and he wondered if she would recall the charming five-petal blue blooms with yellow centres that she nurtured at her uncle's estate: the forget-me-not flowers.

John Owen lowered the lens and whispered, 'I'll withdraw now my dear Amalie, parting is such sweet sorrow.'

EPILOGUE

Present-day

They say forgiveness is to set the prisoner free and acknowledge that prisoner was me, but my bitterness runs far too deep.

As far as Mengele is concerned, my source tells me that after several months on the run, convinced his capture would mean a trial and a certain death sentence, he was assisted by SS members that enabled him to travel to Genoa where he obtained a passport under the alias "Helmut Gregor", and he allegedly sailed to Argentina in 1949.

A Nazi sympathizer housed him in Florida Este and by 1958 he had remarried whilst on holiday in Uruguay and then bought a house in Buenos Aires. It was alleged he began practising medicine, without a licence of course, and along with several other doctors he was brought into question on suspicion when a teenage girl died at his hands after an abortion. He was released without charge. I heard he eluded extradition even though Wiesenthal and Langbein discovered Mengele's divorce papers which led them to an address in Buenos Aires. Apparently, even though an arrest warrant was drawn in 1959, Argentina refused to cooperate because Mengele was no longer living at the address listed on the document. Mengele had already fled to Paraguay by the time it was approved. Yet by 1960, I wasn't the only one that wanted Mengele. West Germany offered a reward for his capture and his face was in a variety of newspapers that wrote about his wartime activities. Various aliases enabled the fugitive to elude capture, but it wasn't until 1969 he jointly purchased a farmhouse in Sao Paulo, Brazil.

Wiesenthal is convinced Mengele is still alive and his current reward stands at $100,000. But for now, I'll take satisfaction in hearing he suffered a stroke whilst swimming and drowned; he had a better death than he deserved.

So what do you define as evil? How do you think Josef Mengele became the evil Doctor of Auschwitz? His prolonged successful evasion of capture, aided by his wealthy family and loyal friends, only added to the mystique and fear among survivors.

I try to keep a Pollyanna-ish persona, but as I told you before, this world is fiction and made up of all kinds of contradiction. I wear this cross around my neck because, although I'm Jewish, my father was Catholic, and it symbolises not only the oppression we Jews experienced but is a reminder of a wonderful man. It hasn't burnt through my skin as of yet. You see, I'm split in two. I'm divided, but unlike William Blake, the poet, painter and printmaker, I do not feel I'm losing my artistic abilities.

"Futurity is before me like a dark lamp."

***

"There is always some madness in love. But there is also always some reason in madness"

Friedrich Nietzsche

WHAT INSPIRED AMALIE

Whilst Amalie does not claim to be an academic piece of nonfiction, it is a story based on some facts. At the time I started Amalie, Holocaust denial was being reported with greater and greater frequency despite the number of memoirs being published and the airing of hundreds of programs about the prisoners, the camps, and newly discovered material relating to the Nazi's Final Solution. Sadly, that denial is still prevalent today.

Organisations worldwide deny the very existence of the gas chambers used for mass genocide and the crematoria that could burn thousands of corpses in a single day. Denying these facts would be minimising the atrocities committed by the Nazis against Jews and other "undesirables". With the advent of the internet, those that perpetuate the lie of denial now have the ability to try to manipulate public opinion and turn conspiracy into hate. Misinformation about the Second World War, and many other historical events, has become all too easy to access. Every year we lose more and more of the survivors of those events; those who can correct the record and expand the knowledge of history.

It is now more important than ever to spread the evidence-based truth as not only a reminder but also a remembrance of the families and descendents of the survivors.

Amalie, as a character, was born when I studied Anne Frank whilst still in school. She was about the same age as Amalie during the outbreak of WWII. I often wondered how a child would learn to cope with the dramatic changes brought by the War; I'm not sure I would have been so brave. I also wondered how witnessing such horrific changes would impact a young person's ascension into adulthood.

The Second World War has always been a subject of interest to me, especially as I am an avid collector of Second World War memorabilia as well as a few pieces from the First World War.

Auschwitz is probably most well-known. It's the one concentration camp used as an example in history classes, and one of the main targets of attack. For me, it seemed logical to base young Amalie's start on the road to adulthood in that camp. The horror of life there propelled her to become this incredibly sinister yet charming social climber. It is true in that we cannot identify villains from their appearances. They look like regular people, if by regular I mean like you and I, then you're correct and it played an important role for how she evaded capture for so long. After all, Amalie isn't a monster; with all her brutality and violence she does have some civility.

I also find it extremely fascinating how the world recovered from the Second World War. The fifties were all black and white and then came the "swinging sixties" which remain the defining decade for Britain. Music came into its own with the likes of the Beatles and it was the decade that influenced a lot of young people with revolutionary changes. Unfortunately, I was born a little later on but I find it fascinating none the less and my other half is always popping out typical British iconic influences of which I am absolutely clueless about having missed out on

British culture. As an adult, I believe it to be important to know my history of the country I was born in (Britain) and writing Amalie was an educational experience about our cultural heritage.

Influences that created Amalie: My mother told me that when I was very young my uncle babysat for me and when she asked him had I behaved, he answered "not a peep, she's been watching Silence of the Lambs". You can imagine her reaction – a serial killer in the making. You could say I was influenced from a very young age and Sir Anthony Hopkins remains one of my most respected and admired actors until today. There have been many factors during Amalie's creation and I hope to bring you more stories in the future.

All the best, E.J.

FUN FACT

In Chapter 8, Amalie looked at a painting of her ancestor and his wife in the 1700s. This painting was inspired from the author's own lineage. It is a portrait of Sir George Strickland, 7th Baronet and his wife Elizabeth, daughter of **Sir** Rowland Winn, 4thBt. of Nostell by Arthur Devis. It was painted in 1751 and has traditionally been said to show them in the grounds of Boynton Hall. Sir William Strickland, 1st Baronet was an English Member of Parliament who supported the parliamentary cause during the English Civil War and was Wood's 11th Great Grandfather.

ACKNOWLEDGEMENTS

I owe my thanks to my partner in crime, Cliff, who has been so supportive of me through this journey – thank you for everything.

I'm also very grateful to my first readers, Maureen, Matt, and my wonderful guardian angel, Sue Scott. Without you Amalie wouldn't be what it is today.

www.ejwoodauthor.com

BIBLIOGRAPHY

ALIGHIERI, DANTE, DA, 'So gentle seems my lady and so pure', 1265-1321, *"So gentle seems my lady and so pure when she greets anyone, that scarce the eye. Such modesty and brightness can endure, and the tongue, trembling, falters in reply".(chapter 14)*

Alighieri, DANTE DA, 'Inferno Canto 1', *"through every city shall he hunt her down, until he shall have driven her back to Hell, therefrom whence envy first did let her loose" 'Therefore I think and judge it for thy best Thou follow me, and I will be thy guide, And lead thee hence through the eternal place".(chapter 39)*

Allen, Woody, WA, *"Of all human weakness obsession is the most dangerous" (chapter 25)*

Auschwitz: The Camp of Death." Holocaust Teacher Resource Center. N.p., n.d. Web. 13 Nov 2011. Holocaust Teacher Resource Center, *"Before dawn, the prisoners were roused from their overcrowded wooden beds for roll call" (Chapter 2)*

https://bit.ly/3k8q0YU

Bauer, Yehuda, (born April 6, 1926) is a historian and scholar of the Holocaust

"Thou shalt not be a victim, thou shalt not be a perpetrator, but, above all, thou shalt not be a bystander."' (chapter 42)

Blake, William, WB, 'Auguries of Innocence" l. 1 (ca. 1803)' *"To see a world in a grain of sand, and a heaven in a wildflower" (prologue)*

Bryant H. McGill, "No one is more insufferable than he who lacks basic courtesy". (chapter 6)

Campbell, Duncan, 29 July 2008, 'Billy Hill biography remembers one of Britain's best known gangsters' – *via* www.theguardian.com, *"I was always careful to draw my knife down on the face, never across or upwards. Always down. So that if the knife slips you don't cut an artery. After all, chivving is chivving, but cutting an artery is usually murder. Only mugs do murder. (chapter 27)* https://bit.ly/3dwcYTu

Christie, Agatha, AC, 'Poirot – The Mysterious Affair at Styles', 1920, *"It is one thing to know that a man is guilty, it is quite another matter to prove him so." (chapter 7)*

Christie, Agatha. AC, *"Any woman can fool a man if she wants to and if he's in love with her"* *(chapter 36)*

Churchill, Winston, WC, Sandringham, Broadcasted, 06-02-1952, *"It is with the greatest sorrow that we make the following announcement. It was announced from Sandringham at 10.45 today the 6th of February, 1952 that the King who retired to rest last night in his usual health passed peacefully away in his sleep, earlier this morning".* Radio broadcast

"During these last months, the King walked with death as if death were a companion, an acquaintance whom he recognized and did not fear. In the end, death came as a friend and after a happy day of sunshine and sport, and after "good night" to those who loved him best, he fell asleep as every man or woman who strives to fear God and nothing else in the world may hope to do". (chapter 14)

Dan Scott, DS, 'Sir Winston Churchill, – Painter

and Prime Minister', August 21, 2019, *"what are you hesitating about?"*, *she took that brush and swept it across the canvas with large ferocious blue strokes and with that Churchill wrote, "I seized the largest brush and fell upon my victim with berserk fury. I have never felt any awe of a canvas since".' (chapter 8)* https://bit.ly/3s3GyUy

Earthly Mission, 'Cockney rhyming slang', *"The language was invented in London in the 1840s by market traders, costermongers (sellers of fruit and vegetables from handcarts) and street hawkers." (chapter 11)* https://bit.ly/3dwcdtJ

Ernest Hemingway, *"Only those who are prepared to go too far can possibly know how far they can go." (chapter 31)*

Fielding, Steve (2008b). The Executioner's Bible: The Story of Every British Hangman of the Twentieth Century (Kindle ed.). London: John Blake Publishing. *ISBN 978-1-8445-4422-6. "avoid attracting public attention in going to or from the prison, and he is prohibited from giving to any personal particulars on the subject of his duty for publication." (chapter 13)* https://bit.ly/2NKjuLu

SS-Obersturmführer Franz Hössler, FH, 1943, *"I am Franz Hössler, I am in charge of the economic function of the camp and on behalf of the camp administration,   I   bid   you   welcome",* https://bit.ly/2NoLdld

SS-Obersturmführer Franz Hössler, FH, 1943, *"This is not a holiday resort but a labour camp. Just as our soldiers risk their lives at the front to gain victory for the Third Reich, you will have to work here for the welfare of a new Europe. How you tackle*

this task is entirely up to you. The chance is there for every one of you. We shall look after your health, and we shall also offer you well-paid work. After the war, we shall assess everyone according to his merits and treat him accordingly. Now, would you please all get undressed? Hang your clothes on the hooks we have provided and please remember your number. When you've had your bath, there will be a bowl of soup and coffee or tea for all. Oh yes, before I forget, after your bath, please have ready your certificates, diplomas, school reports and any other documents so that we can employ everybody according to his or her training and ability.", (chapter 2) https://bit.ly/2NnCO1s

General von Stulpnagel a Nazi commander in Paris, 'Copy of a report to Berlin', *"We Germans must number twice the population of our neighbours. Therefore we shall be compelled to destroy one-third of the population of all adjacent territories. We can best achieve this through systematic malnutrition – in the end far superior to machine guns. Starvation works more effectively especially among the young."* (chapter 4) https://bit.ly/3k69Mzi

Hill, Billy, BH, memoir "Boss of Britain's Underworld", 1955, *"I was always careful to draw my knife down on the face, never across or upwards. Always down. So that if the knife slips you don't cut an artery. After all, chivving is chivving, but cutting an artery is usually murder. Only mugs do murder".* (chapter 27)

Hitler, Adolf, AH, 03-10-1941, 'Broadcast to the German People On The Winter Help Scheme', *"I have come here today to deliver a short introductory address on the Winter Help Scheme. This time it was particularly difficult for me to come here because in the hours in which I can be here a new, gigantic event is taking place on our Eastern front. For the last forty-eight hours an operation of gigantic proportions is again in progress, which will help to smash the enemy in the East. I am talking to you on behalf of the millions who are at this moment fighting and want to ask the German people at home to take it upon themselves, in addition to other sacrifices that of Winter Help this year." (chapter 3)* https://bit.ly/3pCP0Zg

Hitler, Adolf, AH, 'Hitler's last public radio speech: GERMAN COMPATRIOTS NATIONAL SOCIALISTS', *"I expect every German to do his duty to the last and that he be willing to take upon himself every sacrifice he will be asked to make; I expect every able-bodied German to fight with the complete disregard for his personal safety; I expect the sick and the weak or those otherwise unavailable for military duty to work with their last strength; I expect city dwellers to forge the weapons for this struggle and I expect the farmer to supply the bread for the soldiers and workers of this struggle by imposing restrictions upon himself; I expect all women and girls to continue supporting this struggle with utmost fanaticism." (chapter 4)* https://bit.ly/37wVl24

Plato, *"The measure of a man is what he does with power" (chapter 42)* https://bit.ly/2M8PyZh

Shakespeare, William, 'Romeo and Juliet', 1597, *Parting is such sweet sorrow. (chapter 43)*

Shakespeare, William, WS, 'The Merchant of Venice', *"If you poison us do we not die? And if you wrong us shall we not revenge?" (chapter 33)*

Simpson, 'Forty Years of Murder: An Autobiography', p. 206., *"Christie claimed that the four different clumps of pubic hair were from his wife and the three bodies' police discovered, but only one sample matched on the bodies, Ethel Christies." (chapter 13)* https://bit.ly/3btSE2K

UN Secretary-General António Guterres, AG, 'Anne Frank House', *"It would be a dangerous error to think of the Holocaust as simply the result of the insanity of a group of criminal Nazis. On the contrary, the Holocaust was the culmination of millennia of hatred; scapegoating and discrimination targeting the Jews, what we now call anti-Semitism". (chapter 4)* https://bit.ly/2ZzT5CQ

Wilde, Oscar, OW, *"The only way to get rid of temptation is to yield it." (chapter 10)*

William, Robert, RW, "Dabbs" Greer, American character actor, *"I guess sometimes the past just catches up to you, whether you want it to or not". (chapter 26)*

Wikipedia, 'The first Manifesto of Surrealism', 1924, *"Sade is surrealist in sadism". (chapter 8)* https://bit.ly/2NmXjeF

Miscellaneous

"Remember the badge, have you already put on the badge? Before leaving the building, put on the badge!"

"We've done wonders since the war and now we're blowing our own trumpet for a change," the radio sounded. *(chapter 11) Radio broadcast*

"A few days by the sea is a thing tackled by different people in different ways: to some, it is a panic-stricken rush to the railway station with bulging suitcases (chapter 12) documentary

Unknown, Pinterest, *"Yesterday you said hi to me and I died."*

"Secrets of the Clermont Con", DailyMail, 23rd July, 2007. https://bit.ly/3dthYbH

Boothby, Robert Boothby, RB, Baron Boothby, Wikipedia. https://bit.ly/2NKWL28

Slim, Amarillo, A.S, "Sometimes the lambs slaughter the butcher", chapter 38 page 230.

Printed in Great Britain
by Amazon

13687370R00162